Soul Taker

Soul Taker

CELIA REES

Hodder
Children's
Books

A division of Hodder Headline Limited

A Catalogue record for this book is available from
the British Library

ISBN 0 340 87817 7

Typeset in Bembo by Avon DataSet Ltd,
Bidford-on-Avon, Warwickshire

Printed and bound in Great Britain by
Bookmarque Ltd., Croydon, Surrey

The paper and board used in this paperback are natural recyclable
products made from wood grown in sustainable forests.
The manufacturing processes conform to the environmental
regulations of the country of origin.

Hodder & Stoughton
A division of Hodder Headline Limited
338 Euston Road
London NW1 3BH

For Catrin – my special adviser

1

Grey flesh crept back from teeth exposed to the roots in a permanent grin. Bone showed, white tinged with green, below a nose rotted to a snout. Gore ran in streaks down wrinkled cheeks and furrowed chin. Grey hair hung in clumps like mildewed candy floss.

Lewis James's own face floated round and white, with dark holes for eyes, red hair sticking out, every bit as scary as the Halloween fright masks. He stood, hands spread on the dark reflecting glass, trying to see past himself, past the witches on broomsticks and the jagged grins on the shiny orange pumpkin balloons, through the dancing skeletons, around the candle skulls and into the shop itself. He did not want to go in while there were still customers and Mr Ladslow was leaning on the counter talking to a woman.

Lewis hunched inside his parka and retreated, stepping away from the shop. It was late, maybe too late. He should have come straight from school, not wasted time nervously drifting round the town. He stood on the pavement, undecided. He could go, leave now, but he had an appointment. It would be wrong not to keep it. The bell above the door tinged and the woman came out. Lewis was just about to follow her down the street when a voice said:

'Mr James? Right on time . . .'

Lewis turned to see Viktor Ladslow, the owner of Toys'N'Gifts, smiling at him. The town hall clock struck the hour. Five o'clock. Not as late as he thought. The dark comes early in late October.

'Come in, and welcome.'

Mr Ladslow turned the 'Open' sign to 'Closed' and held the door for him. Lewis walked past the smiling man and into the shop. He had no choice.

The interior was a cunning mixture. 'Something For Everyone', the sign above the door read, and Viktor Ladslow was as good as his promise. The Halloween theme was continued inside. Fright masks leered down from netting webs; witches hung from the ceiling, riding their broomsticks across the toy section. Beneath their black silhouetted shapes, carved wooden toys shared shelf space with the latest figures from films. Hand-stitched teddies sat next to Barbie dolls. Traditional board games were stacked under racks of CD-Roms and computer consoles. Trays of plastic, trashy pocket money toys lay on top of glass cabinets stocked with boxed collectables.

Mr Ladslow's shop contained other things besides. Recently he had introduced several lines designed to bring in a new clientele. Beyond the serving counter was a second chamber heavy with the smell of incense. Wooden shelves held scented candles, trays of crystals, displays of jewellery. A cork board advertised various services: astrology, clairvoyancy, alternative healing, hypnotism and tarot readings. One of these notices had prompted Lewis's visit.

He had visited the shop many times. He had been going there ever since he was a little boy. Ladslow's, as it was known, had occupied the same corner spot on Market Square for decades. Lewis had never been in here on his own like this though, only when other people had been there. Being the only one in the shop made him feel self-conscious. This part, with its piles of glassware and tarot cards, made him especially nervous. He pulled his coat close, careful to keep to the centre aisle and well away from the delicate displays in case he knocked something over.

'Go through, go through,' Viktor Ladslow murmured, his voice as dark and smooth as his silky beard and moustache.

A beaded curtain hung down over a narrow doorway which led to the back of the shop. Above the arch a notice read:

Entrance Free – Just leave some happiness!

The top of the doorway was so low Lewis had to duck and his shoulders almost filled the narrow space, forcing him to step sideways. The long passageway beyond was lined with shelves and glass display cases which contained all kinds of toys: carved Punch and Judies, wax-faced dolls, puppet theatres and steam trains. These were clearly old and not for sale. Each one had a little label, stating type and date, hand written in small black writing.

'An idea I have for a toy museum,' Viktor Ladslow said by way of explanation. 'As you see, I have an extensive collection. It would be nice to show it off.'

Lewis stopped in front of three tall wooden cabinets. He glanced towards them, trying to see into their darkened glass-fronted interiors.

'Edwardian amusement machines. I found them rotting on an abandoned pier and restored them myself to full working order. Would you like to try?' Ladslow brought out three large copper coins from his waistcoat pocket and handed them to Lewis. 'Penny in the slot.'

Lewis fed one big coin into the first machine. To begin with nothing happened, then the whole interior was lit with an eerie blue grey light, and Lewis realized he was looking at a scaffold. Little figures came to life. A hooded hangman stepped forward to tighten the noose round the murderer's neck, a priest crossed himself. These two stepped back and the trap door opened with a clack. The rope went taut. The figure jigged on the end and was still.

The second scene was entitled 'French Revolution'. An aristocrat knelt in front of a guillotine. As Lewis pushed the penny home, the blade descended with a thunk and the head rolled into a basket leaving a bloody stump. The crowd waved as the executioner reached down and held up his dripping trophy.

The third tableau lit up red. Flames flickered up dungeon walls, across various instruments of torture. An iron maiden gaped, arms opened wide to display her bloody spikes. A figure stretched on the rack opened its mouth to scream as the wheels turned and clicked. The dungeon master's arm jerked up and down, dipping tongs into ruby coals, quenching iron on skin.

Each scene lasted a minute at most before the glass box began to darken and the machinery inside whirred the figures back to their starting places. The detail was so perfect: the clothes the figures wore, the tiny beads of sweat, the expressions on the small carved faces. Lewis wondered what would happen if he fed more pennies in, would it be the same again, or would the scene move on to some subtle variation?

'A little gruesome, perhaps,' Viktor Ladslow said at his side. 'But such simple entertainments hold no fear for children these days, what with video games and all the horror films they watch.'

Lewis nodded, there was no denying that these things were pretty tame stuff. Nevertheless, there was something sinister about these dark little worlds where small busy figures worked miniature scaffolds, delved in bloodstained baskets and endlessly acted out scenes of horrible cruelty against slimy dungeon walls. He suppressed a shudder. Somehow they were much creepier than the average horror film.

'Still, you have not come to play with the toys,' Viktor Ladslow beckoned him on. 'You are here for quite a different purpose. This way, please.' He swept a second beaded curtain aside. 'This is where I hold my consultations.'

Ladslow's toy shop was an old building. Half-timbered beams showed black against white-washed walls and ran low across the ceiling, forcing Lewis to duck again as he entered the back parlour. The room was small inside, comfortable and cosy. A real fire flickered in the grate and a table lamp in the corner cast a rosy glow. A couple of old velvet-covered armchairs and a matching settee stood grouped close around the open hearth. Against one wall stood a narrow wooden table, the top inlaid with different woods, the legs thin and spindly. Ladslow went over and pulled this out into the middle of the room, then he placed two straight backed chairs either side to face each other.

'Take off your coat,' he said to Lewis. 'Make yourself at home.'

'Where shall I put it?' Lewis asked, struggling out of his parka.

'Anywhere is fine.'

Ladslow indicated the room with a sweep of his arm and watched, hands in pockets, as Lewis looked around for somewhere to stow his stuff. Viktor Ladslow was tall, slightly built, but not skinny. Under his brocade waistcoat he wore a spotless white linen collarless shirt, with the sleeves rolled up to show sinewy dark arms. His black trousers were soft wool and hung loose, held up by a wide leather belt with a carved silver buckle. Lewis turned away, feeling big, scruffy, clumsy, and more awkward by the minute. When he dumped his rucksack, everything spilled out. Lewis scrabbled to put it all back, fingers like sausages. He propped the bag against the settee, leaving his coat and scarf draped across the worn velvet arm.

'Come over here and sit down.'

Ladslow went to the table and pointed to the chair opposite his. Lewis eyed it doubtfully. It looked distinctly spindly and Lewis was big. His mother said he was 'well covered', 'big boned', 'big for his age', but that was not what the kids said at school. They called him fat. 'Fatso', 'tubs', 'fat boy', 'lard boy', 'lard arse', were just a few of his nicknames. Lots of nicknames, no friends. That was one of the things which had brought him into Mr Ladslow's sitting room.

'Don't worry,' the man smiled as though he could read his thoughts, 'the chair is sturdier than it looks. Now what is it to be? Crystal, palm or tarot cards?'

'Crystal,' Lewis mumbled, and the blood rushed hot to his skin.

'Very well.' Ladslow took a silver key from his pocket and opened a tall cupboard. The wood looked old, blackened by time, and the door panels were thickly carved with strange devices. He reached inside and took out a spherical shape, shrouded in deep blue velvet. 'Have you brought the money?'

Lewis reached into the pocket of his 'Waist 40' jeans and brought out three crumpled notes, two tens and a five. He put them on the table and sat down. The chair creaked, but held. This was it now. There was no going back.

Lewis was not very good at ages, but he would have judged the man sitting opposite him to be in his mid forties. Certainly there was no white or grey in the black hair which swept straight back from the high wide forehead. Ladslow's lean dark face narrowed below jutting cheek bones to a jaw and chin covered in a dark beard, the hair carefully shaved and shaped, cut and clipped, sculpted close to the skin. He looked rather fierce, an impression reinforced by a thin nose, hooked and hawk-like, curving like a beak above his black moustache and full lips. A single gold hoop in his left ear lobe accentuated his gypsy looks. Ladslow smiled and Lewis quickly looked away, not wanting the man to think that he was staring.

'Have you a silver coin?' Ladslow asked, holding out his slim long-fingered hand, palm up.

'I don't know . . .' Lewis reached awkwardly into his jeans again and came up with a twenty pence piece. 'That do?'

'Admirably. Cross my palm. That's it.' His hand closed on the coin. 'I give such offerings to charity, but it is still the custom.' He took the velvet hood off the crystal ball and looked down into it. 'Now. What do you want to ask?'

'I – I,' Lewis paused as all the things he wanted to ask: 'Will I be thin?', 'Will I be popular?', 'Will girls like me?' fled from his head.

The man seemed to understand. He smiled again and looked up. His eyes were large and very dark, almost black,

8

deep and reflecting at the same time, like the crystal.

'You must have a question in mind,' he prompted gently. 'You must have something to ask, if you are to receive an answer.'

'OK, OK.' Lewis shifted about on the narrow chair. The frank scrutinising gaze was edged with amusement, as though the man might be laughing at him, and that made him even more uncomfortable. He was blushing again. The crystal showed his cushiony face flushed peony red, clashing with his hair. 'Err, what – what is, what will happen to me?'

'When?' The man's eyes remained on him. 'Now? Today? Tomorrow? In the future?'

'The future.' The chair creaked as Lewis leaned forward. 'What will happen to me in the future?'

The dark gaze held his for a moment and Lewis's fingers gripped the table's edge, leaving prints on the polished surface. Then the man shifted his focus away from Lewis and down into the crystal's blank surface.

Somewhere in the silence a clock ticked. Seconds stretched to minutes as the man stared on, unblinking, his eyes moving slightly, his thin face expressionless, masked in concentration, as he scanned the crystal's surface as if he were reading a screen. Lewis looked too, but could see nothing. Just his own face reflected in the bulging glass, grotesque and ugly, like in the back of a spoon.

At last the man withdrew from the crystal sphere and turned his attention to Lewis again.

'What? What did you see?' the boy asked eagerly.

'Nothing.' He gave an elegant shrug and hitched his white sleeves back from slender dark wrists. 'I saw nothing.' His smile widened at the impact his words had: at the boy's alarm, the way he stared back like a stunned calf. He let out a tinkling metallic laugh. 'No. I don't mean you will get knocked down by a car or drop dead tomorrow.' He folded his arms. 'You will live a good long life. You'll have a career, a successful one, with money, a house, a car. But—' he paused, catching Lewis with his big dark eyes again, 'what I meant was, other than that, I saw more of the same, more as you are now. A sad and lonely boy turning into a sad and lonely man.' Suddenly he leant forward, holding Lewis with his black gaze, focussing on him, reading the boy's blue eyes in the same way as he read the crystal. 'Is that what you want from the life to come? Is that what you want to happen to you?'

Lewis shook his head 'No' to both questions.

'Do you want your money back?'

Lewis shook his head again, the tears of disappointment welling up inside him, pricking at his eyes, cutting off his voice. He turned his head away so the man couldn't see how much he wanted to cry.

'A deal's a deal,' he managed to mumble.

'It is, isn't it?' The man swept a lock of black hair back from his prominent widow's peak. 'I'm glad you see it like that, Lewis. If you had demanded your money back I would have been disappointed, very disappointed. I can help, you see.'

'How?' Lewis looked up in surprise. The man smiled at the sudden hope surging into the dark blue eyes. 'With that?' Lewis pointed a broad finger at the crystal.

'No,' the man shook his head, laughing again, 'the crystal, the tarot, can only reflect and show what is, or what will be, they cannot change destiny – only the questioner can do that for him or herself. I sense you want to change. You do not want to carry on in this way now. Is that not so?'

Lewis nodded.

'Tell me,' Ladslow went on, leaning back in his chair, regarding Lewis over steepled fingers, 'what would you give to change from what you are, to what you want to be?'

'Anything,' Lewis said quietly, looking away from the man down to his big podgy nail-bitten hands. 'I would give anything.'

'Anything, eh?' Ladslow's thin black eyebrows rose, creasing his high white forehead. 'There is much that can be done for a boy who is prepared to give anything. In that case, perhaps I can help you.' Ladslow leaned forward now, resting his hands on the table, slim fingers laced together. 'But all I can do is help you to help yourself. There is no magic involved. Do you understand me?'

Lewis nodded again, although he was not quite sure what the man was getting at.

'Very well.'

Ladslow rose from his seat, his manner suddenly brisk and businesslike. He took the crystal ball, shrouded once

11

again in its velvet cover, back to the cupboard and returned with a pile of leaflets.

'Read these,' he said, handing them to Lewis. 'You have been neglecting yourself. Think about your appearance. That may seem trivial, but it is not. How you appear to others shows a great deal about how you are inside. I'm not saying it is going to be easy. . .' His appraising eyes flicking over Lewis, seemed to say: overweight, badly dressed, generally dishevelled, this boy is a mess. 'The key is to start small,' he went on, 'change one thing at a time, starting with the most possible. You will find one change naturally leads to another. A few basic goals can be achieved immediately.'

'Such as?'

'A good hair cut, some new clothes. You'd be surprised at how different such simple things can make you feel . . .'

'I'd need money for that,' Lewis interrupted, eyes cast down, big shoulders slumped: this was hopeless.

'Maybe I can help with that as well.' The man stood up. 'How would you like a Saturday job?'

'I thought you had someone . . .'

Lewis remembered seeing a boy behind the counter on previous visits to the shop. Older than him, maybe seventeen or eighteen, thin and pale looking, with long fair hair pulled back in a ponytail.

'I did have, but,' Ladslow gave a shrug, 'he has let me down. He has not turned up for two weeks and I have heard nothing from him. We are coming up to a busy time:

Halloween, Guy Fawkes, then Christmas, of course. So, you see, I have a vacancy. You can start straight away. I need someone for tomorrow.'

'I'd have to ask my mum.'

'Ask her then. The job is yours if you want it.'

'Yeah, yeah I will. Thanks, Mr Ladslow.'

Lewis put out his hand, smiling for the first time, and his face transformed. Ladslow smiled back. The boy's eyes were large and fine, an unusual shade of deep grey blue, verging on purple. Tame the auburn mane, slim down the bloated cheeks, remove the heavy jowls and double chins, he might even be handsome.

'Don't thank me yet,' he said. 'Take tonight to read, reflect, think about what I have said.' He shook Lewis's hand, his fingers felt thin and cold but his grasp was hard and strong. 'If you are still interested after that – and if you want the job – come back in the morning.'

2

Lewis's elation lasted all of two minutes. It lasted for precisely as long as it took him to cross Market Square and see who was standing outside McDonald's. Most of his class, and a few from the year above. This was the Friday night gathering place. The place where the whole crowd of them met before going off to wherever they went: cinema, club, party. Lewis stepped into a shop doorway, where he could see them but they couldn't see him, feeling sick, like someone had punched him in the stomach. Jennie Mitchell was with them. He could see her long denim legs, her high-heeled boots, the gleam of her leather jacket. Her short blonde hair shone white in the street light, swinging round her face as she turned to laugh at something someone said. If she was there, Ross Horton would be, too. Sure enough an arm went round her and their faces merged as the boy pulled her to him.

'You don't love her. Not like I do.'

Hatred and envy burned in Lewis's blue-eyed stare, only to be extinguished, almost instantly, by the usual flood of self-pity. He shrank back into the shadows, pulling his hood up, shutting them out until the excited voices thinned, telling him they had gone and it was safe to go on. Only then did Lewis emerge into the cold thin rain and trudge off, shoulders hunched, his massive thighs squeaking together.

The very picture of misery. Viktor Ladslow looked down as the little scene played itself out, leaving the square empty and dark like one of his tableaux. He held the boy's scarf, picking off red hairs as bright as copper wire. He would do well, very well. Viktor Ladslow smiled. The boy was just perfect for his purposes but he could not linger here, thinking about what was to come, wasting time. Putting the scarf aside, he went downstairs and put the strands of hair into a little plastic envelope which he placed in the big black cupboard. That would keep, he thought as he turned the key. Right now, he had a long journey to make. Pressing business which had to be taken care of before he could begin on a new project.

Lewis did not miss his scarf until he got home.

'Lewis, it's late. Where have you been? I've been worried. Where's your scarf?'

'I – I don't know. I must have left it somewhere—'

His mother's tirade of concern changed tack.

'Your Gran knitted that specially – it took her ages – never mind the cost of the wool – you're so careless – always been the same – and you need a scarf on a night like this . . .' She reached up to take his coat. 'You'll catch a chill.'

'For God's sake stop fussing over him, Lil. He's sixteen, not six.' His father turned from straightening his tie in the hall mirror, his eyes slitted against the smoke curling up from the cigarette clamped between his teeth. 'You're ruining him. Look at him. Great fat pudding!'

He turned back to admire his own reflection, smoothing back his thinning red hair, straightening the lapels of his expensive jacket. Lewis got his hair colour and height from him, but there the resemblance ended. Alan James was slim built with pointed features. His eyes were brown and hot, like a fox. Bronze hairs bristled across his upper lip and down the sides of his mouth to his chin.

'I'm off down the pub.' He picked up his mac and headed for the door. 'Don't wait up.'

'But, Alan, what about your tea?'

'I'm going for a curry with the lads.' He glanced at his son standing at the foot of the stairs. 'Give it to the human dustbin.' He grinned, thin lips pulled back to show rows of white teeth above his narrow jaw line.

The door slammed on his wife's reply. Through the distortions of the ribbed glass door, she watched him walk away, not moving until his footsteps began to fade. He never took her out with him any more. Never took her anywhere. 'Do you think I want to be seen with that?' She could almost hear him say it. They were nearly the same age but – she caught her reflection in the hall mirror and touched the frizzed ends of a grown out perm – the years had been less kind to her. Her once bright blonde hair was grey-streaked and colourless.

Alan kept himself smart, spent a lot on his clothes. He'd kept himself trim but she just couldn't seem to get her figure back after Lewis. She dressed for comfort now, in shapeless dresses and elasticated skirts purchased from Oxfam or discount stores. She did not like to ask Alan for the money to buy anything from any of the decent shops. He had a cruel tongue and would use it, offering to get her a three man tent from the camping shop, or saying that he could not afford to have her re-upholstered.

It was her fault. She'd let herself go, she knew that. Being in the house all day hadn't helped. She'd given up work when Lewis was born and Alan would not hear about her going back. 'What for?' he said, 'I earn plenty.' She used to knit and sew, do a bit of handicraft, but she didn't even do that now, all she seemed to do was eat and watch the telly. Alone, or with Lewis. Alan hardly ever stayed in with them. Home from work, wash and change, and straight out, night after night. They more or less lived separate lives. Still, her crumpled brow cleared as she looked at her son. There was always Lewis.

'Fish and chips tonight. Fat chips, mushy peas and crispy batter, just how you like them.' She smiled at him and her faded face regained a hint of its former prettiness. 'Treacle sponge to follow.'

Lewis nodded. They always had fish and chips on Friday

and always homemade, never from the chip shop. Mum was a good cook. Even Dad had to admit that – on the rare occasions he stayed in long enough to eat with them.

'OK.' Lewis went up the stairs. 'Call me when it's ready.'

Lewis sat on his bed for a moment, then he got up and locked the door of his room. He opened his school bag, took out the leaflets that Mr Ladslow had given him, sat back on his bed again and began to read through them. The first one was all about diet and nutrition and being a vegetarian. He put that in the bin, being a veggie did not appeal to him: 'rabbit food' was what his mother called it. He picked up the next: 'Yoga for Health and Fitness'. That looked quite interesting, then he heard his father's laugh yelping in his ear, saw his mocking grin. 'Yoga? You? You can't even see your feet, let alone wrap them round your head!' That went in the bin as well. He picked up the last one. 'Change Your Life – For Good.'

'Decide what you want to change. Take a long hard look at yourself . . .'

Lewis stood up and took off his clothes, stripping to his underpants. He made himself look in the mirror, something he rarely, if ever, did. He was tall for his age, a little under six foot, but this made his problem worse, not better. He was huge. Flesh girdled his face, chins looping down so he had no neck. Fat hung in folds on his chest, making it look like he had breasts. He wanted to turn away, but made himself stare on. His belly sagged, thick pads creased across his back, forming handles where his waist should be; 'jugs' is what the kids called them, another nickname from school. His buttocks were monstrous, spilling out of the baggy white Y-fronts his mother bought from the market. His thighs were chafed on the insides where they rubbed against each other, even his knees were fat. He lowered himself back onto the bed again and covered his face with his hands. He looked like a sumo wrestler. It was hopeless.

Sumo wrestlers. Lewis remembered an article he'd read somewhere. He sat, fingers laced in front of his face, thinking about it. They look that way because that is what their sport demands. They are immensely strong, and fit, they eat to stay big. When they give up the sport, they become normal men again.

Q: How do they do that?
A: Discipline: mental, physical – and diet.

Lewis sat up and fished the pamphlets out of the bin, flattening them out. Maybe there was something here after all. As he read on, hope, a feeling he had hardly ever known before, began to quicken and grow inside him.

'Lewis?' His mother was rattling the door handle. 'What are you doing in there? I've been calling and calling you. Your tea's ready.'

'I don't want any.'

The words were out of his mouth before he'd had time to consider what he'd said. There was silence. Then his mother's voice came back, squeaking through the door in a mixture of dismay and astonishment.

'But it's your favourite! I cooked it specially. You have to eat!' The tone turned to a wheedling whine. 'You can't let good food go to waste . . .'

She sounded so hurt, so surprised, he began to go to the door. Then he checked himself. He was still in his pants. What would she think about that? He had become so absorbed in thinking, studying, filling in the self-appraisal sheet, that he'd forgotten her, the time, everything – even to be hungry. Besides, he couldn't give in now, just when he'd got started. 'Don't put it off,' Ladslow's pamphlet said. 'Change starts now. Today. This minute.'

'Are you poorly?' his mother asked. 'Have you got one of your headaches again?'

Yes. That was it! If she thought he was sick, she might just leave him alone.

'Yeah,' Lewis replied, trying to sound ill.

'I'll bring you something up. Some paracetamol and a hot drink with honey and a little snack to help it down . . .'

'No!' Lewis said loudly and then dropped his voice. 'I just want to sleep. I – I've already taken something.'

'If you're sure . . .'

'I'm sure. Goodnight, Mum. See you in the morning.'

His mother stayed outside for a little longer and then sighed and turned away from his door. Lewis heard her going downstairs, her tread heavy on every step. He almost never lied to her, and he knew he ought to feel bad about it, but he didn't feel guilty at all. He had a strange feeling, like butterflies round his heart, like something big was starting. Tomorrow he would go back to Ladslow's shop, he would take the job. It would be part of the new life he planned for himself. The changes he intended to make started now. It was down to Mr Ladslow that he had even got this far, but this was just the beginning.

Lewis set the alarm, he wanted to wake up early, and then he lay on the bed, eyes closed, thinking that keeping his appointment with Mr Ladslow was the best decision he ever made. At first, when the man didn't tell him anything interesting, he'd thought it was a waste, but now he felt differently. It was not enough just knowing what the future might hold, what mattered was the ability to change it, to change your own destiny, that was what Lewis considered to be such excellent value.

But the £25 was for the consultation only. Anything else was over and above, and Viktor Ladslow was not a man who gave things away. That night Lewis slept soundly, undisturbed by dreams, premonitions, or any other indication that the debt he owed would have to be paid with something far more precious than money.

3

The night was cold, very cold. Cold in the Midlands where Lewis lived; he would wake up on the first day of his new life to find the ground hard, grass as brittle as glass, the trees rimed with frost. It was even colder in Scotland. By the early hours the freeze was biting deep, making the pavements glisten and glitter, making them slippery and treacherous. It was a hard night to be out on the beat and you would think the cold would send folk home, but no. The pubs had decanted into the clubs and from there people spilled out into the street to fight, to mug, to fall down drunk. It was Friday night and Glasgow was buzzing, whatever the wind chill factor.

By five o'clock things had begun to quieten down. PC Sutherland was just thinking about finishing his rounds and heading back to the station for a big breakfast fry-up, when he heard a shout for help. It came from the basement of one of the all night multi-storey car parks. Probably someone had found their car gone, or the window smashed and the stereo ripped out.

The stairwell smelt of urine and when he got down to the lower ground floor there was nobody about. He cursed to himself. This would probably turn out to be a waste of time and he could be halfway back to the station by now.

He looked around. There were only one or two cars left, only one or two daft enough to park down here. He shone a light, probing into the dark corners, that was when he saw it. He thought for a minute that the thing he'd caught in the beam of his torch was a mannequin, dumped as some sick kind of Halloween joke, designed to frighten people. Probably fooled whoever had raised the alarm, too. Whoever had yelled out had done a bunk, either feeling too foolish to stick around, or not wanting to get involved. Certainly, there was no one here now.

The policeman went over, edging nearer. He was wrong. This was no shop window dummy. He was looking at a naked body. White. Male. Young. Not much more than twenty years old. Clean shaven – including the head.

There were no signs of obvious injury, no physical indications as to what might be wrong. PC Sutherland felt the neck. There was a faint pulse. He stood up, radioing urgently for help. Could be drink, drugs, some kind of substance abuse. Sutherland took off his coat and wrapped it round the boy on the ground, tucking it in under the torso. As he did so, a fragment of memory kicked in. There had been a circular from down south, somewhere in England, enquiring about missing persons. He'd have to check when he got back to the station, but he was pretty

23

4

Mr Ladslow did not seem at all surprised when Lewis turned up the next day at his shop. He showed the boy how to work the till, staying beside him for the first few customers. After a while this wasn't necessary, Lewis was a quick learner, good at maths, fast at adding up. By late morning Viktor Ladslow could go into the back, leaving him in charge. Lewis used slack periods to get to know where everything was, get to know the stock. Not that there were many times like these, most of the time the shop was pretty busy.

Everything went fine, could not have gone better, until halfway through the afternoon when Jennie came in with her friend Carrie. Caroline Kirkpatrick. Lewis began to say 'Hello' but Carrie walked straight past him. Her brown eyes, cold as pebbles, looked through him as if she had never seen him in her life before, even though they had been in the same class since Year 4 in junior school. Lewis just stood there, mouth open, humiliation staining his cheeks. Jennie noticed the snub and smiled at him.

'Hi, Lewis. I didn't know you worked here.'

'I – I – I – I . . .' the blood beat in Lewis's face. As if the whole situation was not embarrassing enough, he had somehow developed a stammer. 'I've only just started . . .', he said when he could get the words out.

'Come on, Jen.' Carrie turned impatiently back for her friend. 'Are we going to do this, or what?'

Jennie half shrugged and Lewis dropped his gaze away from the perfectly oval face framed by silver blonde hair, the greeny blue eyes smiling into his, away from her beauty.

'Have to go. We've got an appointment. For the tarot.' She smiled her slow lopsided smile. 'See you later, Lewis.'

'Yuh – yuh – yuh – yuh—' he stuttered, then gave up and just nodded.

The two girls went through to see Mr Ladslow for a joint consultation. They emerged after about twenty minutes or so, Carrie's dark face flushed and excited as she came back into the shop. She completely ignored Lewis again, going straight past him, chatting to Jennie. Her friend listened in silence. She seemed subdued, pale and preoccupied, but she still managed a little wave and a quick half smile on her way out of the door.

'Pretty girl.' Mr Ladslow stroked his silky black moustache. 'They both are, but particularly the blonde one. Do you know her?'

Lewis could not trust his voice. He just nodded.

'Do you like her?'

Lewis nodded again.

'Would you like to know her better?' Ladslow laughed as hope and disbelief passed like clouds across Lewis's eyes. 'Of course you would. Stupid question. Tell me, Lewis,' Ladslow regarded him steadily, suddenly serious, 'what would you give for a chance with her. Anything?'

'Anything? I'd give everything! Everything I have, everything I am, for just one chance!' The boy's eyes glowed with desire and sincerity, but gradually the light died. 'She would never look at me. Not in a million years. Such a thing is impossible. Anyway,' he looked at Ladslow suspiciously, 'what could you do about it?'

'Oh,' Ladslow shrugged and smiled his enigmatic smile. 'You never know. I could help. If you want me to.'

'How?'

'You'll see.' Ladslow's eyes glinted with something like mischief, his smile widening in the face of the boy's obvious disbelief. 'Trust me. But first you must do something for me. Tonight is Halloween . . .'

Ladslow stopped as real alarm flared in Lewis's face, and then he laughed, a metallic scatter of sound.

'No spells, no tricks. All I meant was I have to change the window display ready for Monday. Replace the skeletons and pumpkins with fireworks for Guy Fawkes. I have to do this tomorrow. Sunday is the only time I've got and I have many other things to do. If you promise to come in and help me,' he gave an elegant shrug, 'I'll see what I can do about Jennie.'

Lewis's face cleared. He gave that dazzling smile again as he held out his hand.

'You've got a deal!'

'Yes,' Ladslow smiled back, grasping Lewis's hand in his hard cold grip. 'I rather think I have.'

Lewis spent the rest of the afternoon in the back of the shop constructing a Guy Fawkes guy. He worked in the Modelling Room, a big work room which ran the length of the furthest part of the building. Mr Ladslow used this as his workshop, he had explained to Lewis when showing him round earlier. Here he repaired broken toys and made up kits. Here he also designed his own toys and sculpted his own models. He was working on an idea for remote controlled action figures, programmed by a microchip and powered by small high-energy batteries. Once he got the design just right he was hoping to apply for a patent and sell the idea to a big toy company. His grandfather was a gypsy, he said, he had made toys and marionettes, so it was in the family. Lewis was not surprised to find that Ladslow had gypsy blood. The man's slim, lithe, wiry build, his dark hair and eyes, his skill with his hands, all proclaimed his ancestry.

Lewis had asked to see some of the toys he made, they sounded interesting, but Ladslow had shaken his head, saying that there was not time now, maybe tomorrow. Meanwhile, Lewis could look at what was out but was not to touch anything, and he was not to enter the Finishing Room.

Ladslow indicated a shut door leading off the Modelling Room, next to the stores which held the stock. It held delicate machinery, Mr Ladslow explained, several special prototypes in different stages of development, so Lewis was not to go in there without permission. Lewis agreed readily enough. After all, he had free run of the place. He could go anywhere else he wanted; make tea, coffee, play with anything that took his fancy. This one restriction, this single prohibition was certainly not too much to ask.

Lewis found the things he would need to make the guy already set out: straw for the body, sacking for the face and head, an old black hat, an old pair of trousers. Mr Ladslow said to look for any other clothes he might want in the 'lost property' box.

The first thing Lewis found in there was his own scarf. He put that on one side. He was not particularly fond of it, but Mum would be mad if she walked past the shop and saw it wrapped round the neck of a Guy Fawkes. He found a T-shirt, a jumper with holes in it, and a zip-up hooded top. The top looked quite new. Lewis shook it out. Pale green with a mauve stripe and a surfing logo on the chest and the back. Expensive. Lewis was not very into fashion, but he knew that items like that did not come cheap: it must have cost upwards of forty or fifty quid.

There was no name inside, but there was something familiar about it, he was sure he had seen someone wearing it. The memory trembled on the brink of recall and was gone. Maybe someone at school, or one of the skaters who hung round the multi-storey car park, they wore gear like that. Lewis thought of wearing it himself, but he couldn't even zip it up, it was way too small. Whoever had worn it before was of a much slighter build. He returned the jacket to the box. It was too good for the guy and whoever owned it might come back and claim it. Guy Fawkes would have to make do with a holey jumper.

Lewis was so involved in his design that he did not notice the time. He was surprised to find it was well past five when Mr Ladslow came to see how he was doing.

'That's admirable!' he said as Lewis jumped to his feet. 'That will do very well. I brought you a mask, but I see you don't need it.'

'I – I used some modelling paint. I hope you don't mind . . .'

'Not at all.'

Lewis had painted the face on to the sacking. Red mouth set in a sneer inside a goatee beard. Large dark eyes, sad and defiant at the same time, glaring out from under a black slouch hat.

'He looks a bit like me!' Mr Ladslow laughed, picking the guy up and setting him on a bench.

'Oh, I'm sorry.' Lewis was horrified, that had been the last thing on his mind. 'I didn't mean—'

'Don't worry,' the man shook his head, 'I like him very much. You worry too much about upsetting people. I'd say you were very talented—'

'Oh, I don't know . . .' Lewis blushed, not used to receiving praise.

'If I say you are — you are. You have to learn to take compliments. Here,' Viktor Ladslow reached into his trouser pocket and took out a couple of notes, 'this is what I owe you.'

Lewis looked at the money, disbelievingly, not knowing what to say. It was far more than he had been expecting for working that day.

'You earned it,' Viktor Ladslow said. 'Don't you think you deserve it? And there is also tomorrow. You haven't forgotten our deal?'

Lewis looked at him blankly.

'Guy Fawkes? The window display?' Ladslow smiled at the boy's incomprehension. 'You promised to come in and help me . . .'

'Of course. No. No, I haven't forgotten. Forget my head if it wasn't screwed on, that's what my mum says.' Lewis grinned wryly as he picked up his scarf. 'What time do you want me to come?'

'In the afternoon. About two?'

'That'll be fine. See you then, Mr Ladslow.'

Viktor Ladslow let the boy out and returned to his work rooms at the back of the shop. He walked past the guy still propped up on the bench: he had meant what he said, the boy had talent. Indeed, he had more than that. He showed a great deal of potential. He was a good worker, very intelligent and he learnt quickly. Very promising. He had learnt by trial and error that high IQ facilitated transfer, made the whole process easier. Viktor Ladslow smiled, pleased with his selection. His interest in Lewis James went far beyond his usefulness as a shop assistant.

He took a key from his pocket and opened the door to the Finishing Room. This room was large, lit from above, like a studio. A long work bench ran down the central space. This was set out with apparatus: vices, lathes, cutters and guillotines, bunsen burners, magnifying lenses mounted on tripods. Against one wall was a large sink, a small furnace and kiln, oxyacetylene cylinders, welding and metal-working equipment. At the end of the room was a computer work station set up next to a cutting table piled with bolts of cloth. An ironing board stood against the wall and to the left of this was a store of bins for clay and shelves holding moulds and all sorts of modelling materials: from blocks of wood and plaster of Paris to polyurethane foam and experimental plastics designed to reproduce exactly the feel and quality of human flesh.

Viktor Ladslow turned on a Bunsen burner and adjusted the flame. He reached for a lump of pure beeswax, sniffing the spicy honey smell as he broke the block into a crucible and set it to melt. He took from his pocket two small plastic packets. Each contained strands of hair. One set so red that they might have been threads of copper, the other so fair they might have been silver. The girl was a stroke of genius. That was another thing that made Lewis such an excellent choice.

He dropped the hairs, one at a time, into the pale golden

melted wax and turned off the flame. While he waited for the wax to cool, he set out on the work bench the other things he would require. Little glass beads for eyes, one set blue, the other green, sculpting tools for the fine shaping and carving, a jeweller's eye glass to get the small details right. As he did this, he muttered and hummed to himself in a language not immediately familiar, the words indistinct. It might have been an old song he was chanting, or it might have been some kind of spell.

5

Lewis got up early on Sunday morning and went out to the garage, careful not to make too much noise. He did not want to disturb his father, who valued his lie-in, or alert his mother, who might start asking what he was doing.

The car was parked in the drive which made everything easier. He opened the garage door and stepped into the oil-smelling, grimy half-light. From now on he would go everywhere on his bike. It might not seem such a radical decision, but his first goal was to improve his fitness and 'the longest journey starts with just one step', that's what one of Ladslow's pamphlets said.

Lewis found the bike under a heap of broken deck chairs and old garden furniture and dragged it out into the back yard. It was a full-sized mountain bike. Dad had got it off some bloke at work. It had fallen off the back of a lorry most likely, still it was a good make.

The bike had been a little too big when he first got it and Lewis had felt self-conscious, scared of falling off. Dad had had a real go about that, taunting him, saying he needed stabilisers, accusing him of being a baby, riding like a girl. Mum had worried herself sick that he would end up under a bus, and then the front wheel had got a puncture. That was five years ago. The bike had been in the garage ever since, growing rust.

Lewis collected what he needed from the jumble of tools on the dusty work bench. He had bought a cycle repair kit on the way home and spent the previous evening studying the instruction manual.

The first surprise was how much taller he had grown. The saddle would have to be put up considerably if he was to ride it comfortably. Lewis turned the bike upside down onto the saddle and handlebars so he could repair the puncture and see what else needed doing. The second surprise was how easily he did that, almost one-handed. The third surprise was the one his father got when he finally emerged from the back door.

'What the hell do you think you're doing?'

'I'm doing up my bike.' Lewis carried on cleaning the chain and seized-up gear parts in warm soapy water. 'What does it look like?'

'What for?'

'Because I'm going to ride it.'

'Cuh!' his father snorted derision. 'Where? You're going to look like a flipping circus bear!'

Lewis said nothing, just shrugged his large shoulders.

'Yeah, well,' Alan James said into the silence, scratching at the red stubble peppering his chin. 'Don't you come to me wanting it put back together. That bike'll be in bits from now to kingdom come!'

Lewis ignored him and carried on with what he was doing, not turning round until he judged that his father had gone. His mother was peering out of the kitchen window, waving a J cloth at him, trying to get his attention. He ignored her, too.

Lewis worked on all morning, re-assembling the gears, repairing the tyres, scrubbing off rust with a wire brush, getting busy with the chrome polish. Sometimes he hated his father. No. Not sometimes. All the time. He wished he could be less foul-mouthed, more polite, more considerate and refined. Lewis spun the wheels and watched them flash in the sun. He wished his father could be more like Mr Ladslow.

'Lewis? Dinner's nearly ready, dear.' His mother had come out now, he could feel her hovering just behind him. 'Brr!' She shivered. 'It's a wonder you've not caught your death out here.' Lewis turned, surprised. He hadn't even noticed that it was cold. 'Time to get cleaned up now, anyway. Just look at you!' Her face puckered with disgust. 'You're filthy.'

'OK, Mum. I'll be there in a sec.'

Lewis lifted the bike and put it back on its wheels, adjusting the saddle to his present height. He stood back, wiping his hands on a rag, admiring his morning's work. The tyres were pumped and plump, fresh oil coated the working parts, the paintwork gleamed and the chrome was shining. His old bike looked good as new.

'What do you mean, you're not eating meat?' His mother stared at him in horror; she could not have been more shocked if he had announced that he intended to ride naked down the street. 'You need the protein, you're a growing lad!'

'If he grows much bigger he won't be able to get in through the door! Don't fuss over him, Lil. If he wants to starve, let him.' His father sawed off another bleeding slice from the Sunday roast and dumped it on his own plate. 'All the more for me.'

Lewis said nothing. Once he'd got it out of the bin, he'd read and re-read Ladslow's booklet about vegetarianism. It had begun to make sense to him: if he was seriously to lose weight he could not eat any kind of animal fat, but he did not expect his parents to understand. He did not argue, just helped himself to more vegetables. He refused pudding too, making do with a wizened apple from the fruit bowl. Then, when his parents had settled down, his father to sleep behind his paper, his mother to watch the Sunday afternoon soap round-up, he announced that he was going out.

'Where?'

'To Mr Ladslow's. He asked me to help him and I thought I'd give the bike a spin.'

'Well, all right.' His mother's eyes flicked from the screen to him and back again. 'But you be careful. And don't be late back.'

She kept her voice low, careful not to disturb her husband, anaesthetised by Sunday dinner and a couple of pints down the club.

'I won't. Don't worry, Mum. See you later.'

Lewis couldn't wait to get out of there, away from the television murmur, his father's snore, the rustle of the paper as it slid to the floor. He let himself out, closing the door on the tired, centrally-heated air trapped behind double glazing, with its familiar Sunday smell of burnt meat and gravy, his father's cigarettes. He jumped on his bike and pedalled off into the bright autumn afternoon. The cold air smelt new to him. It smelt good. It smelt of something he had rarely known before. It smelt of freedom.

'Lewis! So glad you could come.' Viktor Ladslow smiled in welcome. The boy was standing taller, straighter, just this made him look at least a stone lighter. 'Put your bicycle in the back. I will let you in.'

Lewis walked down the alleyway by the side of the shop. Viktor Ladslow met him by a door in the wall and let him into a large yard. At the back of this was a ramshackle building, about as big as a double garage.

'Your bicycle will be safe in here.' Ladslow opened the doors. 'You can't be too careful, so many thieves about,' he stroked his silky black moustache. 'And that's a nice model.'

'What's that?'

Inside was an old-fashioned gypsy caravan, its curved barrel shaped top almost touching the roof. The front was ornately carved, the shafts sticking out, little steps leading up to the painted doors.

'My grandfather's vardo, his living-waggon. He was of pure gypsy stock. It should have been destroyed, burnt when he died, but there was no-one among the gadze to observe the custom.'

'The gadze?'

'That is what the Rom, the Romanies, call non-gypsy people.'

'Is that who you get the fortune telling from?'

Ladslow laughed. 'Not from my grandfather. I told you, he was a toy maker. His mother, though, my great-grandmother, was a famous soothsayer. Most fortune tellers base their skills on intuition, observation, and people's gullibility, but she had the gift, apparently. Other gypsies would travel miles to consult her, and that is the real test.' He paused, looking at the waggon. 'My grandfather settled here. Married a local girl, gave up the travelling life, so I am only a quarter Romani.'

'Why did he stop? Travelling, I mean?'

Ladslow laughed. 'He fell in love and never went on the road again, made his living here instead, making toys, and he had a certain skill with horses.'

Lewis nodded. The town had a race track and there were quite a few racing stables hereabouts.

'His name was Grigore Lazarovich. He came from Eastern Europe, from Serbia originally. He changed his name to Gregory Ladslow, easier for the gadze to pronounce. When he had enough money, he bought this shop. When he died, my father took over. Then me. Small town shopkeepers,' he gave a little half-smile. 'A long way from our gypsy origins.'

'Why are the caravans supposed to be burnt?' Lewis asked.

'Well, after the person dies, it should be set alight along with all their belongings, so that their ghost can leave. Otherwise the ghost stays around to bother the living, that's what the Romanies believe. But,' he shrugged, 'as there was no-one here to do that for him, the custom was not observed.' He looked thoughtful. 'I'm glad in a way. It would be a shame to destroy such a beautiful thing. Don't you think?'

Lewis nodded.

'Would you like to see inside?'

'Oh, yes!' Lewis wanted to very much but hadn't liked to ask.

Ladslow opened the doors onto a perfect little interior world: beds, a table, chairs, and a little cooking range. Copper pans shone. The surfaces were free of dust, the floor freshly swept.

'I keep it clean for him. Gypsies are fanatical about cleanliness. I sometimes sit in here, light the oil lamp, wonder what it was like to live a free life . . . Come. Enough. We have work to do but first I have some things to show you.'

Ladslow shut the little doors and led Lewis into the side of the shop. As they passed the toy collection, he showed

Lewis some of the toys his grandad had made: puppets carved from wood, clowns and harlequins, with strings to move feet and hands, cars and trains hammered from bits of tin.

Ladslow pointed out the detail in each one, praising the skill involved, and then he took Lewis to the Modelling Room to see the figures he himself was working on. These could not have been more different. The old man's toys had a timeless quality, made of the simplest materials, worked in ways that had not changed for centuries. Ladslow's figures were made from the latest materials and contained complex computer gadgetry. They were light years ahead of the hand-held marionettes – strictly twenty first century.

Lewis was so fascinated, he even offered to help. He was good with computers and loved technical gizmos. People thought he was clumsy because he was big, but he wasn't really. His thick fingers had a delicate touch, as long as no-one was watching, as long as there was no-one there to make him nervous. Oddly enough, Mr Ladslow did not make him nervous.

The toy maker shrugged and said he'd see about him helping, meanwhile there was the window to do. He led Lewis through the beaded curtain and into the front of the shop where the back of the window was open. Ladslow had cleared the Halloween display to make way for Guy Fawkes Night. The guy Lewis had made the day before sat next to bundles of twigs and sticks, there was a sack of crisp curling autumn leaves to strew across the floor and a big bag of conkers. Fireworks, boxed and single, lay spread out ready to go in the window.

'These are dummies, of course.' Ladslow picked up a rocket. 'We can't put live ones on display. Tell me, Lewis, do you like fireworks?'

Lewis nodded. Not that they had ever had any at home. No-one had ever invited him to their garden either but, when he was small, he used to go to the display at the local fire station with his mother.

'Remind me to give you some. There are always lots left over. Now this window...'

Lewis nodded again. Letting them off on his own would be really sad, but he didn't like to refuse, that would be ungrateful and it was a kind thought. Perhaps he could have some rockets. Lewis bent down and picked one up while Mr Ladslow told him what to do. He held it by the thick wooden tail, feeling the weight of the fat packed shape under the plastic cone. Letting off a rocket or two wouldn't be so bad. He liked rockets.

Mr Ladslow went off to do work of his own and pretty much left the boy to it. Sunday was the only day he had to make his models. He did not just work on his own toy designs, he explained to Lewis, he also made figures to order for special customers. These could be up to life size. People were prepared to pay hundreds, thousands even, for the right thing. It was a very lucrative part of the business.

Lewis settled into his task. He enjoyed doing things like this. He had quite a flair for design and was doing Art for

GCSE and, after Maths, it was his favourite subject. He marked out the glass, fixing on letters and plastic star bursts. He stuck rockets to the wall, fanning them from big to small, beneath them he began to construct the bonfire and, as he did so, his thoughts drifted and settled on Jennie.

She did Art, too. She was in his class. One day she had modelled for them, fully clothed, of course. She had sat in the middle, ignoring the boys and their stupid remarks, as the group set up their easels around her. It was the happiest afternoon of Lewis's entire life. He could look at her: at the way her hair fell over her forehead to her finely arched eyebrows, ponder the exact colour of her greeny blue eyes, admire the sweep of her long dark lashes. He could follow the line of her cheek to the curve of her lips, see how the depression in her lower lip echoed the slight cleft in her chin. He could draw the line of her jaw, study the soft hollow at the base of her neck. He could stare as intensely and as long as he liked without anyone making any kind of comment. He memorised her, every detail printing itself inside his head, until he could close his eyes and see her still.

His portrait had been by far the best. The teacher had praised him, brought Jennie over to see it. She had paused by his side, leaning over his shoulder, so close he could feel her breathing, and had gazed at herself for a second or two. 'That's good, that's very good,' she'd said, smiling her enigmatic half smile.

Memory painted his face as red as the crepe paper flames

licking round the feet of the guy. Lewis felt himself being watched and blushed deeper still. He turned to find Mr Ladslow looking at him, studying him as intensely as he had studied Jennie.

'I – er, I was just – er—'

'You have done very well. I couldn't have done better myself,' Ladslow stroked his close-cut beard, hiding his smile, but lights danced in his big dark eyes and Lewis wondered if he could read minds as easily as palms or cards. 'I usually have a cup of tea around this time, I was wondering if you would care to join me?'

Lewis ducked out of the window and stood before him.

'Stand up straight.' Ladslow looked him in the eyes. 'You are tall, almost as tall as me and how old are you? Sixteen? You will be a tall man. Use your height. Be proud of it. Don't slump and slouch, keep your head up, in line with your spine.' Lewis felt himself straighten under the man's gaze. 'That's it,' he laughed, and patted the front of Lewis's shirt, 'there you are, you've lost a stone already. Did you read the pamphlets I gave you?' Lewis nodded. 'Come with me, then. I have some other books which you might like to see. I think they may be of interest.'

'Does it work? All this stuff?' Lewis asked, looking up from the volumes Ladslow had given him.

'In what way?'

'What I mean is,' Lewis sat forward in his chair, his blue eyes intense, 'is it really possible to change?'

'Of course,' Mr Ladslow put down his cup. 'If you want to enough up here,' he tapped his forehead, 'in the mind. It's all a matter of discipline.'

'Yes, but . . .'

' "Yes, but . . ." ' Ladslow gestured with his hand, 'is a phrase I don't like. It introduces excuses. "Yes, but" are the worst words I ever hear. "Yes but . . ." means you are not ready for it.'

'I'm sorry . . .' Lewis felt confused, not sure what to say.

'That's OK. Just dismiss those words from your mind and we will get on fine.'

'So what do I do?'

'Whatever you want to.'

Lewis frowned. They seemed to be going round in circles.

'That's the point,' Ladslow went on, 'don't you see? You can do whatever you want, be whatever you want to be.'

'But how?' Lewis cried in anguish, almost shouting.

'Find what it is that wants changing – and change it, that's all.'

'But,' Lewis spread his hands in a gesture of despair, 'there's so much that's wrong, so much to change, I – I'm not sure where to start.' His big shoulders slumped, his hands fell back to rest in his ample lap. 'It's impossible. Like climbing Everest.'

'Nothing is impossible. Even climbing Everest. Plenty of people have done it.' Ladslow thought for a moment. 'In fact, that is a pretty good analogy. Tell me, Lewis, how would you go about such a project?'

'Climbing Everest?' Lewis shook his head.

'Well, I'll tell you, shall I? First you would have to get fit because an expedition like that would be physically challenging. Then you would have to learn how to climb and become very good at it, because Everest is a very difficult mountain. Then you would have to get the money together to fund yourself, by sponsorship, or earning it, then you would have to find and join an expedition . . .'

'But that could take years . . .'

'Yes, of course. That's the point I'm trying to make. But it's possible. And if climbing Everest is the one thing you want to do above everything, you are going to think, when you are standing at the top of it, that it was time and money well spent. Do you understand?' Lewis nodded slowly, he was beginning to see what Ladslow meant now. 'You can't get there all at once,' the man went on. 'Start small. Be methodical. Break up your old routine and replace it with another. If you're not happy about the way you look take more exercise, change your diet – what's the matter?'

Lewis was thinking of his other problem. His face fell back again into its usual lines of mournful defeat.

'It's my mum. She's going to be a pain. If I don't eat, she goes mad. She says I'm starving myself, making myself ill. She's already got upset about it.' Lewis thought back to the battles they had already had: not eating tea on Friday, refusing chips last night, and meat today. 'I don't want to give in but I don't want the rows to get any worse.' He looked down at his hands. 'She has enough to put up with.'

'I'm not telling you to starve yourself, am I? Give her a list of what you want to eat: fresh fruit, vegetables, rice, pasta. You can eat as much as you want of that. She probably doesn't much care what you eat, as long as you eat a lot of it,' he smiled. 'Mums are like that.'

'Yours, too?' Lewis looked up, a brilliant smile transforming his face.

'Mine, too. She wouldn't let me get up from the table unless I'd eaten my own weight. At your age I was fat, like you.'

'Really?'

'Yes, really. So if I can do it, so can you.'

'Do you believe that?'

'Of course. It's a long road and it won't be easy, but I think you have started already.' Ladslow stood up. 'Enough for today. Take these books. Read them. They will help you. Change one part of your life and you will find change occurring in another, and another.' Ladslow grinned, his teeth showing white against his gypsy dark skin and black moustache. 'Soon you will hardly recognise yourself.'

6

Ladslow was right, it wasn't easy, but neither was it as difficult as Lewis thought it was going to be. He took the books home and read them carefully. And then, without even really thinking about it, he found a notebook and started writing down the thoughts he encountered in the books he read, thoughts which interested him. He began to get up an hour earlier than usual, not to meditate, that sounded pretentious, but he could think in the quiet of the sleeping house and concentrate his mind on the day ahead.

He went to school on his bicycle. On the first day it took him nearly half an hour and he arrived red in the face, puffing and sweating. By the end of the first week it was taking him twenty minutes, by the end of the next week he had got his time down to ten.

He found an old fitness manual in his dad's sock drawer: *Canadian Air Force Exercises*. Dad swore by them, not that he ever did any, his slack muscles and little pot belly were a witness to that, so he didn't notice when the book went missing. Lewis added sit-ups and press-ups to his early morning thinking routine. In the evening he began to go running, sneaking out of the house when his parents were safely watching the telly.

He began by running round the block. It wasn't far, but the first time he was sick and nearly passed out. He was sick the second time, too, but gradually it got easier, until he found himself adding more streets to his circuit, then the park. Soon he was going mornings as well. He looked forward to it.

Food had been less of a problem than he had anticipated. Mum had accepted his list of preferred items with the minimum of grumbling. Dad had sneered about 'foreign muck' and 'rabbit food', but he rarely ate with them anyway. Mum was actually persuaded into thinking this new diet was a good idea and had joined in, this made everything a whole lot easier. By the end of the second week, Lewis had taken his belt in a couple of notches, the weight was falling off him. Mum's face was looking a little less puffy, her colour was better, so maybe it was doing her good, too.

Lewis certainly felt different, as he cycled off to work for the fourth Saturday. He felt proud, in control, and with this came another feeling, a strange new feeling. For the first time in his life, Lewis James felt powerful.

Mr Ladslow did not say anything, but Lewis could see in his eyes that he was noticing. Part of him wanted Mr Ladslow to be pleased with him, although the man had told him: 'You must do this for yourself. Not anybody else.'

The shopkeeper agreed readily when Lewis asked to go an hour or so early so that he could have his hair cut and do some clothes shopping. Lewis had been watching the boys at school, paying close attention to how they wore their hair, what clothes they bought, how to wear them. He knew exactly what he wanted and where to get it and he had plenty of money; some left from his birthday and he'd done some extra time at Ladslow's. The boy who had worked there before still had not turned up, so Lewis volunteered a couple of nights after school, another Sunday, helping to change the windows, and Mr Ladslow paid well.

The shops were emptying by the time Lewis got to them. Halloween and Guy Fawkes were long gone. It wasn't even the end of November but tinsel glittered in the window displays and 'Jingle Bells' played over the loud speakers, Christmas was coming. It did not take him long to make his purchases. He strode from one rack to another, collecting what he wanted: shirts, trousers, boots, underclothes, piling them onto the counter, looking round nervously, not wanting anyone from school to spot him. His haircut felt funny: layered at the back, longer at the sides, parted high, flopping into his eyes. He flicked back his shiny chestnut fringe and caught sight of his reflection in the mirror; for a moment he genuinely did not recognise himself.

Viktor Ladslow recognised him easily enough from his window above the shop. He saw the boy turn right out of Market Square, carrier bags swinging from the handlebars of his bike, and smiled. So far, so good. He had been right about the boy, he was proving to be an excellent subject: strong-willed and strong-minded as well as intelligent. He was far more suitable than the last one who, despite Ladslow's best efforts, was still proving problematic. And, of course, he had brought with him another dimension. Ladslow looked down at the wax models in the glass-topped box: one male, one female, one red-haired, the other blonde. 'Poppets' was the old-fashioned name for these dolls and they had nothing to do with childhood playthings, they were the stuff of witchcraft.

7

The odd thing, or the odd thing for Lewis, was that no-one at school seemed to notice what was happening to him. It was as though he was part of the furniture, like an old sofa, something everyone skirted round and took for granted.

They used to notice all right. He'd been bullied for years, ever since junior school, everything from name calling and handing over his dinner money to anyone who fancied it, to serious physical intimidation. But that had ceased now. Maybe his tormentors had got bored, or maybe they had grown out of it. Oh, they liked to see him fail in the gym, they liked it when one of the sports teachers went out of the way to humiliate him, then they would all join in. He still took his fair share of comments in the changing rooms and the showers, but he had learnt to keep out of the way, hide in corners, arrive either early or very late, and most of the time they just ignored him.

He had ridden to school on Monday acutely aware of his new clothes, his new haircut, wondering who would be the first to start taking the mick, but nobody did. Their indifference would have upset him before, particularly after all the effort he had made. There would have been a time when he would have been very cut up, torn between the agony of being noticed and the humiliation of being ignored. Now it did not seem to matter. He regarded them all from under his new fringe and just got on with his work. They would notice soon enough and, besides, he was not doing this for them, an inner voice reminded him, he was doing it for himself.

Lewis had a study period that afternoon and, as usual, he went to the library. He registered Jennie as soon as he came through the doors, but went and sat on his own, positioning himself carefully, not too near, certainly not on the same table, but where he could see her, watch her, without being noticed.

The library was quiet. Apart from the librarian in her little office behind the counter, they seemed to have it to themselves. Jennie was leaning forward, silver blonde head bent over a stack of books. She was chewing the end of her pen, staring at a messy spread of papers spewing out of her overstuffed folder. Lewis sat, elbow on the table, hand shading his eyes, watching her through his fingers. She was crying. It didn't take him long to realise. One by one, tears were dropping down onto the page in front of her. She smeared them away with her hand and then gave up any pretence of studying. She uttered a deep shuddering sigh and sat, head in both hands, the tears seeping through her fingers.

Lewis stood up, quite aware that he would most likely be totally blown out, but he left his place and went across to her table.

'What's the problem?' He glanced down at the books spread out on the table. 'Can I help?'

Jennie looked up in surprise and wiped the wetness from her cheeks with her sleeve.

'No. I'm OK,' she started to say, but fresh tears squeezed from the sides as she closed her eyes. 'It's this Maths – I've got to get it in to Blakely by three thirty this afternoon. It's an assessed module and – and – I can't do it.'

Lewis studied the papers in front of her, the mess of half-completed graphs and crossed-out equations.

'It's easy. We did this work last term.' He was in a higher Maths set than her. 'Would you like me to help you?'

She looked up at him, tears magnifying her greeny blue eyes. 'Would you? Would you really?'

'Of course!'

He smiled then and, despite her tears, Jennie found herself smiling back. It might have been out of sheer relief. Lewis James was clever, particularly at Maths, everyone acknowledged that, but it might also have been because she had never noticed he had such a nice smile before, its brilliance was infectious.

'Here. Let me see . . .' He pulled up a chair and sat down next to her. 'Look, it's like this . . .'

He flipped over to a clean page in her refill pad and

began to write figures down in his clear precise hand. Jennie picked up her pen, and then put it down again.

'This isn't going to work!'

Lewis looked up. 'Why not?'

'Because Blakely will know! He did the last time when I used Carrie's. He told me specially, "Do not copy." '

'Who said anything about copying?' Lewis smiled again. 'I'm not going to do it for you. I'm just going to show you what to do. Explain each part and then you do it.'

'But what if I can't?'

Jennie was beginning to panic again, but his large dark blue eyes held hers, helping to calm her.

'What if you can? The secret is to think you can. Lose the negativity. Once you allow yourself to think you can do it, then it comes easy, OK?'

Jennie nodded, still not sure. She hadn't quite thought that way before, but as he went through the module with her, patiently explaining each equation and formula, she found it all beginning to make sense. Her block about the work she'd been set began to disintegrate and suddenly it seemed much easier than she had ever dreamed possible.

'Oh, Lewis,' she said when he had finished, 'that's brilliant! I understand it now. Thanks, thanks a million . . .'

She looked up at him, into those purple blue eyes, and began to notice other things besides, noticing them for the first time; the glints in his shiny auburn hair, the arch of his dark eyebrows, his pale clear skin: no erupting spots, just a spray of freckles across his nose and cheeks. His wide full mouth, his teeth showing in a white and straight line when he smiled.

She realised with a shock that he was really fit. Now that she had started, she couldn't stop staring at how his round moon face had changed, how the chubbiness had melted away to show the strong bone structure underneath. She glanced at the rest of him. That wasn't bad, either. His checked shirt was tight over his broad shoulders, but he no longer filled the rest of it, his belly was flat above the leather belt of his cords. The material stretched taut across his well-muscled thighs.

'That's all right,' he was saying, 'do you think you can do it on your own now?'

'What?' Jennie focussed back on his face.

'I said, can you get on by yourself?'

'Oh, yes. Thanks, thanks for your help.'

'Do you want me to move over here?' He indicated his books on the desk across from hers. 'Help you if you get stuck?'

'Yes. Sure. Whatever.'

Jennie stared down at the page, trying to collect herself. Fancying Lewis James, what could she have been thinking of? He was working next to her now. Her eyes strayed sideways to his arm lying on the table, almost touching hers: the sleeve folded back over muscular forearms and wide flat wrists. No fat there. No fat anywhere. The Lewis James she had known for years had gone. He was like a completely different person, a stranger, yet someone she knew. Jennie shivered, this was uncanny, like *déjà vu:* the feeling this had happened before, or that something predicted was coming true. He had such lovely eyes . . . Just thinking about them made Jennie feel strange. She shivered, but not from cold, it was as if an electric current was passing through her, she felt it in the pit of her stomach. Just for a moment, she saw other eyes, dark eyes: deep, black and luminous, smiling, full of knowing as they looked up from reading her future, and then in a blink they were gone.

She picked up her pen and glanced at the clock. This would not do. Not do at all. While she sat here dreaming, the deadline was looming. She settled down to work through the sets of calculations, her need to get it finished on time driving all other thoughts from her mind.

When the bell went at 3:20, Jennie had almost finished. She completed the last question and began pulling her papers together.

'Would you like me to check it?' Lewis asked.

'Well, it's a bit late now,' she smiled, 'but, yes, if you like.'

'Good. It's very good,' he said as he looked through. 'There are a couple of mistakes,' he grinned at the stricken look on her face, 'but they're only small. No one gives it in perfect. You're bound to make a few mistakes.'

'Yeah, I guess.' Reassured, Jenny shuffled the papers into order and put them in a plastic wallet ready to hand in. 'I'd never have done it without you, though . . .'

She looked up and was caught again by those dark blue eyes, his mouth smiling at her. How could anyone fancy

Lewis James? How could anyone? How could? He was close now, his chair turned towards her. Their eyes met again. This is the library, she thought. What if my friends see me? What if they do? Jennie leaned forward, closing the remaining space between them, and kissed him on the cheek.

Outside the library's glass doors, Carrie Kirkpatrick's mouth dropped open in amazement. She stood, eyes wide, unable to believe what she'd seen, what she was still seeing. She snapped her mouth shut and grinned to herself. This was good. This was the best. She turned and ran down the corridor, back to her class base, the report already forming in her head, 'You will never believe what I've just seen!' Pause for people to ask, 'What? What?' and then go on to the main event, 'Jennie and Lewis James – in the library – she kissed him!'

The story went fast as fire through Year 11 getting ready to go home from school, the word leaping from the classroom, spreading to the cloakroom, jumping from one person to another.

The crowd had thinned by the time Lewis got to the locker hall, and if people were looking at him, he didn't notice. He was in a dream of his own, a complete daze, seeing through a golden haze. He fumbled the key and opened his door, unable to believe what was happening. He stared into the dark interior, with no idea about what he was looking for. He just stood there thinking, this is better than a lottery win, better than anything, when the steel door slammed shut with a bang, nearly trapping his fingers.

'I want a word with you, you fat git,' a voice said behind him.

Lewis turned. A ring of boys cut him off from the rest of the narrow hallway. They stood, hands in pockets, staring at the floor or the ceiling, striking casual attitudes so no passing teacher would think there was anything going on here. In the middle stood Ross Horton with two of his special cronies.

'Yeah, I want a word with you – fat boy.' He looked around. A couple of others grinned at the insult. He turned back to Lewis, eyes narrowed, face twisted in menace. 'Listen to me,' he hissed, 'you go near Jennie, rubber-guts and I'll . . .'

He glared, leaving his look to finish the sentence. He didn't believe what he'd heard. Carrie was a stupid cow, Jennie wouldn't go near this barrel of lard, but even so, he couldn't let it go. He had his reputation to think of.

'You'll what?'

'This.'

Ross balled his fist and the other boys moved in tighter. The punch was hard and vicious, aimed at the solar plexus. Ross expected his hand to sink into fat gut, but it didn't, it connected with a solid wall. So solid, Ross thought he'd missed and hit the locker door. He expected Lewis to cry out, double up, start to blubber. This did not happen either. The other boy just stood there. His face was not red and about to cry, it remained pale and impassive. Ross bunched his fist again, ready to take another smack. The other lads were looking at him, kind of questioning, and this made him really mad. He was going to smack that big fat mouth. He looked up, sizing his target, and realised, for the first time ever, that Lewis James was taller than him, quite a lot taller; and big, broad at the chest and across the shoulders. Slabs of muscle showed under his open-necked shirt.

Ross's eyes flickered away and his fist uncurled, dropping down by his side.

'Don't go near her.' He squinted up at Lewis. 'Because if I hear anything, even a whisper, I'll have you. Are you listening, fat boy?'

'Yeah,' Lewis replied, 'I'm listening.' He folded his arms. 'Why not now? You and me outside. Fair fight.' He glanced round at the others and then back at Ross. 'How about it?'

Lewis held Ross with his hard flat gaze and smiled. At first, Lewis had failed to recognise the look in the other boy's eyes. Although he had felt it often enough inside himself, he had never seen it in anybody else. Ross, who had made his life a misery, tormented him for years, was afraid of him.

'You ain't worth it.' Ross sneered round, but the other boys looked away, they were avoiding his eyes, everyone knew he was backing down. 'Just if I catch you, I'll—'

'You'll do nothing.'

Lewis stepped forward, drilling each word home with his forefinger into the other boy's chest. Ross was so surprised he stumbled backwards, losing his balance, tripping over the feet of someone standing behind him. He would have fallen sprawling to the floor if one of his mates hadn't caught him. His scowl smothered the sniggers that were breaking out.

'You ain't heard the last of this,' he snarled at Lewis as he pulled himself back upright. 'Not by a long way. I'm telling you: you touch her – you're dead!'

He went off down the locker hall then, punching doors as he went, stalking, stiff-legged, like a dog might walk. Two of his mates followed, but the rest of the boys stayed round Lewis.

One of them even patted him on the back and said, 'Well done, mate. He had it coming.'

'Yeah,' another one said, 'ain't many got the guts to front Ross.'

Lewis nodded and smiled but he was glad when they drifted away. He leaned back on his locker, hands on his knees, eyes closed. Now it was all over, he couldn't believe what he had done. He was trembling all over and felt like he was going to pass out, or throw up, but he did not do either. He stood up after a moment or so, breathing rhythmically and deeply to centre himself before going to meet Jennie.

8

'I'll see you tonight, then,' Jennie said, when they got to her house.

'What?'

'Outside McDonald's. Eight o'clock.'

It was Friday. All week, in school, out of school, Lewis and Jennie had been seeing a lot of each other. Each night he walked her home and, on the way, they spent time in town, having a coffee, wandering round the shops. He'd even been to her house, helping with homework, keeping her company when she was babysitting, but this would be different. This would be with her friends, other people. Lewis hesitated. He was not sure if he was ready for this.

'Of course,' Jennie looked up at him, 'if you'd rather not. I mean, if you can't be bothered . . .'

'It's not that! Of course I want to. It's just,' he looked away, 'I'm not exactly Mr Popularity. What if your friends start having a go at me?'

'And what if they don't?' Jennie swung open her garden gate. 'Anyway, you've got to come with me. I want them all to know that I'm going out with you. I don't want anyone to be in the slightest doubt.' By anyone she meant Ross. She turned back and said over her shoulder, 'You'd better be there.'

And, of course, he was. The evening was not half as bad as Lewis expected. Jennie was a popular girl and Lewis found himself accepted, part of the crowd. And it got easier: each time they went out, Lewis found himself more at home, more relaxed, more sure of himself with other people. It was almost as if there was someone there with him, coaching him, prompting him, telling him how to act and what to say.

Sometimes, when he was waiting for Jennie, laughing and joking outside McDonald's, a shiver would run down his spine and he would glance across the market place, to the row of bus shelters, just to check he wasn't standing there as his old self: fat and ugly, lurking in a darkened doorway, consumed with jealousy. Then he would look up at the window above Ladslow's shop giving silent thanks. It had all come true, just as predicted. There were never any lights on, but Lewis had the distinct feeling that the man was up there, watching and smiling as though he'd had a hand in what had happened and found it pleasing.

The only people who weren't too pleased were Jennie's best friend Carrie – and Ross. These two drifted together, united by their dislike of Lewis and what they thought he was doing to Jennie. Carrie thought her friend mad, deluded; Ross reckoned 'the fat boy's put some kind of hex on her'. They sat in corners, fomenting hatred between them, staring across every so often, plotting how to get even; but Jennie wouldn't listen and Lewis found it easy to ignore the evil looks coming his way. He did not care what they thought. He was far too happy to worry about those two and after a while he stopped noticing altogether.

Jennie worked on Saturdays, too. She had been taken on for the pre-Christmas rush by one of the big clothes shops in the new shopping mall. This meant that they could spend their lunchtimes with each other. After work, Jennie came to meet him because she finished earlier than he did. Mr Ladslow was quite happy for her to come in while Lewis finished up, but Jennie did not like doing this: waiting in the shop made her feel uncomfortable. Ladslow was always excessively charming and polite to her. His urbane, courteous manner was one of the things Lewis admired, but it cut no ice with Jennie.

'I'm not sure about your Mr Ladslow,' she announced one Saturday when they were leaving the shop, 'I think he's creepy.'

'Really?' This had never occurred to Lewis. 'Why?'

'I don't know,' Jennie shrugged, 'it's just a feeling I get, like caterpillars crawling up my back every time he comes near me. It's like – ' she thought for a moment, ' – that time when I had my fortune done. Afterwards, he helped me put my coat on, held it for me and flicked my hair out of the back of my neck.' She shivered. 'I didn't like that.'

'It's just his way,' Lewis said, 'kind of old-fashioned.'

'It's not just that.' Jennie frowned. 'It was the things he said. Like he knew all about me. Even Carrie said it was uncanny.'

'What did he say about her?'

'Nothing. She wimped out at the last minute, so it was just me. And he knew all sorts of things about what I'm like, about my family, about Ross and me, even you indirectly.'

'Oh?' Lewis was intrigued. 'What did he say about me?'

'Well, I didn't see it as you at the time, but he said I would meet someone who was intelligent, sensitive, considerate and kind,' she laughed, 'therefore obviously not Ross. And it would be someone known but not recognised. And he would be,' she paused, then went on in a rush, 'and he would be my first true love.'

Lewis stopped walking and stared at her, thunderstruck.

'And that's me?'

Jennie looked up at him. 'Of course. What do you think? Come here, stupid.'

Her arms went round him. Her lips were warm, touching his cold cheek, finding his mouth. They stood kissing on the street corner, not caring who passed by, not caring who saw them.

Viktor Ladslow smiled, delighted with himself, delighted his experiment was going so well and dropped the soft silken cover over the two tiny figures locked together in the limpid depths of his crystal ball.

★

'Oh, I don't know . . .' Lewis frowned.

Jennie was babysitting tonight, and had asked him to join her, which was all right. The house was near his, so she'd suggested dropping in on the way to pick up some tapes to play, which was not so all right. It meant she would have to meet his folks, and that was something he had been trying to avoid, but he could hardly leave her standing out in the freezing cold.

'Oh, go on. You aren't ashamed of me, are you?'

Lewis shook his head. It wasn't that. Quite the opposite, in fact. He wasn't sure what she would think of him, the house, Mum and Dad. He wasn't sure how his father would react. Not well, if his response to the news that Lewis had a girlfriend at all was anything to go by.

'Girlfriend? What girlfriend? I didn't even know he had a girlfriend. Cuh!' His father had barked his sharp yelping animal laugh. 'What girl would go out with him?'

'Her name's Jennie,' his mother had replied. 'She works in Miss Selfridge. She's very pretty.'

'Cuh! That's what you think. I'm always saying you need glasses. Or maybe she does.' Dad had gone off on a different tack. 'She must be blind as a bat! She must be to go out with that. I mean, stands to reason . . .'

Lewis cut off his father's remembered remarks, the mocking voice yapping in his head. Lewis straightened his shoulders and pulled himself up to his true height before opening the door. Maybe this meeting would be a good thing. Give Dad something to think about.

Mr James was standing in the hall.

'Hi, Dad. This is Jennie.'

His father's mouth dropped at the sight of the girl, for once he was lost for words.

'Come in. Come in,' he managed to say, standing back so they could enter the house. 'Can I take your coat? Would you like a drink?'

'No, Dad,' Lewis replied, 'we just dropped by to pick up some tapes.'

'What about your tea?' his mother asked from the kitchen door. 'Hello, dear,' she came over, smiling, wiping her hands on her apron. 'I'm Lewis's mum. Lewis didn't say, we weren't expecting you, but you're welcome to join us, more than welcome . . .'

'You just heard him say they weren't going to stay,' Mr James snapped. 'Stop fussing, Lil, for goodness' sake. Now, my dear,' his voice smoothed to oily charm as he put his arm around Jennie, shepherding her into the lounge, 'are you sure I can't tempt you to a drink? Beer? Vodka? Gin? We've got most things . . .'

'No, Mr James. Honestly . . .'

'We've got plenty of soft drinks, love, if that's what you'd rather.' Lillian James glared at her husband. What was he doing, offering spirits to a young girl?

'How about something soft, then?' Mr James went on, ignoring his wife. 'Orange juice? Coke?'

'No, really. I'm babysitting.' Jennie checked her watch. 'I said I'd be there before seven.'

'Where?'

'Percy Road . . .'

'I'll drop you round in the car. No problem.'

'I don't want to put you to any trouble.'

'No trouble. Won't take a minute. Now, how about that drink?'

'Oh,' Jennie gave in, 'OK, then. I'll have a coke.'

'Right!' Alan James rubbed his hands. 'Ice and lemon?'

'Yes . . .'

'Go on then, Lewis!' he turned to his son. 'You heard! Coca-cola for the young lady, ice and lemon, and a beer for me. Make it snappy. Where's your manners?'

His mother sliced the lemon and found ice in the freezer. Lewis went to the fridge to get the coke and beer. When he came back with the drinks, Jennie was sitting on the settee and his father was in his chair, with a stupid grin on his face, asking her to 'Please call me Alan.'

Lewis left them to it and went upstairs to collect the tapes. When he'd got those, they were out of there, lift or no lift.

He met his father just coming out of the lounge, an empty glass in his hand.

'Dad . . .' he started to say, but his father interrupted.

'You've done all right there, son,' he whispered, drawing Lewis across the hall. 'She's a real cracker! Chip off the old block, eh?' He punched Lewis lightly on the shoulder. 'Eye for the ladies, just like your old Dad. Who'd have thought it?' He winked. 'I always said you'd come good. Bit of a late developer!'

68

'Yeah, well,' Lewis looked down, embarrassed. 'We've got to go.'

'I'm giving you a lift.' His father put down his beer glass to make rings on the hall table. 'Hang on. Just get my coat.'

'It's OK. We'll walk. Jennie?' Lewis called into the lounge. 'Are you ready?'

'Yes.' She came out to stand beside him.

''Bye, Mum,' Lewis yelled towards the kitchen. ''Bye, Dad.'

His father opened his mouth to protest once again, but Lewis ushered Jennie out of the house. Alan James ran a hand through his thinning hair, shoulders slumped. Lewis looked back. His dad looked smaller somehow, crumpled and diminished. The door snicked shut and Lewis felt something crack, shift and change in their relationship.

9

Lewis worked for Ladslow every Sunday now. What with going out on weekend nights and Christmas coming up, he needed the money. He was planning on buying Jennie something nice, something really special; but 'nice' meant expensive, and when Ladslow had offered him extra hours in the weeks leading up to Christmas, Lewis had jumped at the chance.

He filled in a couple of nights after school on a regular basis too. The pale blond boy with the pony tail had never come back, leaving Ladslow short staffed at one of the busiest times of the year. Lewis served behind the counter, so Mr Ladslow could be free to deal with other things, like the horoscopes and tarot readings. He wanted to build that side of the business. Saturdays were getting very busy, very busy indeed, but there were no customers on Sunday. Lewis spent the time tidying up, re-stocking, and helping in the work shop. Sometimes Mr Ladslow would take out particular examples from his own collection of classic dolls and show them to Lewis.

Most of the dolls, he said, had never been meant as children's playthings. Indeed there was nothing childlike about them, in appearance they looked like little adult women.

'Look at the workmanship in the clothes.' Ladslow tested the fabric between finger and thumb. 'Pure silk. Hand stitched. And the moulding in the features – beautiful, adorable.' He traced the contours lightly with sensitive fingers as if touching a real woman's face. 'So expressive. Look at the modelling of the lips.'

The way Ladslow talked about them made Lewis feel uncomfortable. He remarked that all the dolls looked the same to him.

'They are not! They are as individual as people!'

Ladslow was annoyed. His voice went quiet, silky with fury; black brows drawn down over eyes hard as onyx marked his displeasure. Lewis apologised. He made a mental note not to criticize Ladslow's collections again.

'The best,' Ladslow explained, having obtained a correctly respectful attitude from his audience, 'the most expensive have their original wardrobes intact, and of course,' his hand rested lightly on a cap of golden curls, 'real human hair, like this.'

These dolls, these fashion dolls, had been made to show off the latest Paris clothes before the advent of magazines. Ladslow had quite a big collection of those but his specialism was in automata, figures moved by mechanical means. Again, these would have been much too expensive and delicate to have been played with by children.

Ladslow sat at the bench for hours, jeweller's glass screwed into one eye, a line of tools ranged at his side, mending intricate clockwork mechanisms. Whether they were over wound or worn out by use and time, he brought them all back to full working order. Lewis admired his skill but he did not share his employer's love for these particular toys. Sometimes Ladslow would wind them up to show Lewis what they did. This was a great honour and Lewis had to fight hard to hide his distaste. He did not want to offend his employer, but there was something unpleasant about the way the eyes on the little figures snapped open and the little mouths gaped to let out strange strangled cries, showing their black insides. Neither did he like the tiny grinding noise the machinery made or the way their arms and legs worked in jerky chopping movements.

Also on Sundays, Ladslow would show off his 'replicates', the battery operated action figures he was hoping to patent. To make them, he utilised the same materials and technology used by the makers of artificial human body parts. The eyes were supplied by an ophthalmic manufacturer. The limbs consisted of silicone rubber and latex foam sculpted and moulded, built up over stainless steel bone and tendon, the movement controlled by complex circuits. Lewis admired the technology, but in some ways he found these scarcely less repellent than their automated ancestors. The finished product was very lifelike; seeing hands and arms lying about sometimes give him a fright. There was something vaguely macabre about the unfinished heads and piles of disconnected limbs, and the faces, although beautifully modelled, were eerily blank. Their limited range of expressions, matched to different digitalised voices, gave Lewis the creeps, and the skin which looked and even felt so much like human skin, was mushroom cold and clammy.

Lewis was quick to learn and good with his hands, his touch deft and assured. Ladslow often left him to do low level assemblage while he got on with his other work: the making of customised models and figures for special orders. Lewis was not allowed to touch these. In fact, much of this activity went on in the Finishing Room, away from the main workshop. The figures could be any size, from tiny to almost life. They were exquisitely worked, making them took many hours of time, and the result was scarily human. They could be made singly, or in pairs or groups to make up 'tableaux vivant': the figures grouped and programmed to perform a series of actions as though they were alive. The tableaux were created by Ladslow round themes specified by the customer. Lewis had only a hazy idea of who these 'customers' were, or what they wanted these things for, but one thing he did know: these personalised grown-up toys cost a great deal of money. So much that Ladslow sometimes spoke about concentrating just on this and giving up the hassle of the shop all together.

Mr Ladslow had come to trust Lewis, giving the boy responsibility, letting him get on independently. Lewis liked that. The toyshop owner had long ago asked him to 'Please call me Viktor.' Lewis could not quite bring himself to do that but he felt at ease in the man's company. Mr Ladslow treated him as an equal, spoke to him as though he was another adult. He was a good listener, too. He had listened patiently to Lewis going on about his mum, his dad, his life in general. He did not interrupt, just let Lewis get it off his chest, but he offered sound advice.

'Your dad is jealous of you,' he'd said, without looking up from his bench.

'How's that?' Lewis had shaken his head, remembering his dad's jeering face. That could not be.

'Think about it. You are young, with your future before you. Full of life, full of energy. He's trying to suck that out of you. It's a kind of violence.'

'He never hits me, or Mum . . .'

'I don't mean that. It's a kind of psychic violence. He's got you under his thumb – you and your mum. He dominates you both completely; he doesn't have to use physical force.'

'So what can I do?' Lewis wanted to know.

'First, remember he is taking your energy because he doesn't have enough of his own. He has to steal it from other people. Also his methods of doing it are very negative: criticism, mockery, undermining everything you do, that is how he seeks to control you. If you feel it happening, put a block on it. Imagine your energy is like water held behind a dam. Don't let anyone mess with the sluice gates. You control the flow. You have to do it, Lewis. You can't be your true self, fully independent, while you let him dominate you.'

Ladslow stopped talking then and got on with his work, but he continued to observe quietly – he liked to see his words working their way deep down into the boy's consciousness. He enjoyed doing that: feeding ideas into his head, and all the time making it seem like Lewis himself had thought them out. It was important for Lewis to be strong. Ladslow had put considerable time and effort into moulding and forming this boy. He did not want his work undermined by someone as poisonous and destructive as his coarse, crass, boneheaded father. Lewis needed to be an individual in his own right, beyond the influence of any other person; any person, of course, other than Ladslow himself.

Their conversations were not limited to Lewis's home life, they delved into everything and anything: life, religion, philosophy. Ladslow was always coming up with interesting little facts, snippets of information on different topics. Sometimes it seemed to Lewis as if the range of his knowledge was limitless. He could not imagine conversing like this with anyone else, certainly not another adult. The teachers at school, even the nice ones, were brisk and distant, and nobody talked that way at home.

Lewis imagined his father must talk in the pub, or when he went down the club, but Lewis could not imagine what about, probably sport. He rarely talked to his son or wife unless, like Ladslow said, to carp or criticise. Mum and her friends confined themselves to gossip and exchanging tips about home furnishing. All she did with Lewis was ask endless questions: 'Where are you going? What are you doing?' These had increased threefold since she had found out about Jennie.'Where does she live? What do her parents do? Why don't you bring her home properly for tea one night?'

Lewis loved his mum, knew she meant well, but sometimes it felt as if he was being crushed between his father's massive contempt and his mother's chronic anxiety. Sometimes he had to escape. Ladslow's place was the perfect refuge from the seismic tensions building in the house. On this particular Sunday, Lewis arrived to find Mr Ladslow busy in the Finishing Room, working on an order that had to be completed soon. Lewis busied himself round the shop: replacing stock and gunning on price labels after their busy Saturday. The work was boring and repetitive, requiring little thought or concentration, but Lewis didn't mind. He liked the peace and quiet of the shop resting after the trading week's activity; he liked getting everything in order, making ready for the days to come. When there did not seem anything else left to do, he drifted through to the workshops at the back to see if Mr Ladslow was ready for a brew.

'Mr Ladslow, would you like me to make a cup of tea?' Lewis rapped on the door of the Finishing Room. When he got no reply he knocked again, harder this time. 'Mr Ladslow?'

There was still no answer. Ladslow must have gone out to the back, or upstairs for something. The door was not quite shut. It gave to the touch. Lewis pushed tentatively and it swung back a little bit. Classical music spilled through the space. Mr Ladslow often had music on while he worked. Lewis pushed the door harder. Maybe the toy maker had become so absorbed in whatever he was doing that he just hadn't heard.

'Mr Ladslow?' Lewis said again, and put his head round the door. 'Are you in here?'

The long whitewashed room was similar to the other work shop but tidier and, if anything, even better equipped. A wide work bench ran the length of it, vices set into it, some of them padded, tools arranged in neat rows. There was a computer station and wide plan drawers, shelves with bolts of cloth and an ironing board. Against the other wall was a big sink and what looked like blacksmithing and metal working equipment, gas furnace and crucibles, welding torch and oxyacetylene cylinders.

Lewis looked around. There was no sign of Ladslow, no sign of anyone at all, except . . .

There was someone in the far corner, sitting against the wall. Someone – or something. Lewis flinched back, the hair rising like fur up his arms, fingers clenching. He ought to get out of there. Right now. But he could not move. He just stood, eyes wide, staring.

At first Lewis thought that he had found a body. He steeled himself, forcing his frozen limbs into action. His sneakered feet squeaked alarmingly loud on the polished tiled floor as he crept nearer to the slumped over figure, his sweating hands leaving palm prints edging the length of the long wooden bench. He approached the place where it lay, propped against the wall: head to one side, eyes closed, long fine lashes showing against milky skin. Lewis took in the high cheek bones and hollow cheeks, the silver gold hairs, fine as emery powder, dusting the slightly square jaw line, outlining the pale sculpted lips. Lewis stood, hand over his own mouth, the only sound his own blood pumping loud in his ears as he looked down at the flaxen pony tail snaking over one shoulder of the green and purple zip jacket, covering up the surfing logo. One arm was curled round a shiny sports bag, the other rested on a painted skateboard. The legs were spread out in baggy skater's jeans. The feet, in Van's trainers, sprawled at 45 degree angles to the floor. Lewis knew who it was. He recognised him immediately. It was the boy who had worked there before. The boy who did not turn up anymore.

Lewis stared on, unable to blink, his paralysed brain gradually taking things in, obvious things, things he would have noticed earlier, straight away even, if he had not been so shocked. The figure was smaller than the boy would have been in real life. Lewis remembered him as being rather tall, nearly as tall as himself, in fact. This figure was about a third of that. He was looking at a replicate. This must be Ladslow's 'very special project'.

Lewis felt weak, his knees buckling, ready to give, his

breath escaping in a snorting gasp of relief. He stood for a moment, trying fully to understand what exactly it was that he was looking at, his mind scurrying to supply some kind of explanation. Ladslow had told him that many dolls were based on real life models. The automated dolls Lewis had seen were made to perform a whole range of activities – walking, skipping, playing musical instruments – so why not skateboarding? It made sense. And yet. And yet . . .

The doll was so perfect. It was as though the boy had been somehow miniaturised. Lewis felt his mouth dry, panic gripping his insides again. Surely that was not possible? He was just about to dismiss the idea as another wild fantasy and get out of there, when something made him take one more look at the boy on the floor. Tears were sneaking in a silver streak down the nose to the side of the mouth. Lewis could have sworn that the face had been dry before. Then the eyelid, pale blue, laced with tiny purple veins, began to flutter . . .

Lewis withdrew from the Finishing Room, backing away slowly from the door, leaving it at just the same angle ajar. His breath coming hard, he groped behind him until he found the solid edge of the bench. He gripped onto that, trying to stop the shaking in his legs, trying to steady himself. There had to be some kind of explanation. Maybe he had seen no change at all, maybe it was an optical illusion. Or maybe it was still activated in some way, a residual charge of electricity left in the circuitry. It could have been programmed to cry, or the tears could have been caused by condensation. He had to get a hold on his own imagination. He'd really had himself going for a minute. Lewis shook his head and felt his heart rate begin to slow.

'Ah, Lewis.' Ladslow's words made him jump again. 'I'm sorry. I didn't mean to startle you . . .'

'Sorry,' Lewis managed to say, 'I was miles away.'

'I've been looking for you. Where have you been?'

The question was neutral. Ladslow's large dark eyes contained no sign of suspicion, or any kind of menace, but Lewis did not want to be seen as a spy and instinct told him that to answer truthfully would be unwise.

'I – I've been in the shop. And then I went to tidy the stock cupboard.' Lewis indicated the door to the right of the Finishing Room. 'It's in a bit of a mess, so . . .'

'Oh, right. That's fine. You carry on,' Ladslow said, smiling. 'Then perhaps you'd like to make a cup of tea. I could do with one, I don't know about you?'

Lewis nodded his agreement. Ladslow appeared to believe him. He accepted the lie completely. In fact, it seemed to Lewis that his explanation had been met with just the slightest hint of relief.

10

Lewis rode home thinking all the way about the Finishing Room, and what Ladslow might be doing in there, but he could come up with no adequate explanation, not one that made sense, anyway. When he got to the house, Mum and Dad were in the kitchen having a row. He stepped into the hall and the exchange of words between them drove the toy maker and his activities out of Lewis's mind.

'What's it to you?' his mother was saying. 'It's not any of our business.' Then, as the front door closed, she added, 'Shh, he might hear you.'

'What if he does?' came the reply, braying and defiant, but as soon as Lewis came into the kitchen, his father went out.

'What were you talking about?' Lewis asked.

'Nothing.'

She turned away from him to carry on getting supper ready. Cold cuts and bubble and squeak, as always. Lewis went to the fridge to get the salad stuff. His mother's lips twitched as she chopped and mashed the vegetables, as though she was carrying on the interrupted argument in her head. Lewis knew they had been talking about him, but what had they been saying? He'd know soon enough.

'She'll dump him, see if she doesn't,' his father announced before Lewis got to the table. 'Stands to reason,' he continued, shovelling up fried potato and cabbage. 'Nice girl like her – attractive – good-looking – what on earth could she see in someone like him?'

'Shh, Alan. He'll hear . . .'

'So what? I'm only saying the truth, aren't I? Leading him up the garden path, that's what she's doing. Someone's got to say it. Couldn't be more clear.'

Lewis came in from the kitchen, bringing a bowl of salad for him and his mother. His father grinned at him, flecks of green showing on his teeth, knowing that his son had heard and not caring, meaning him to hear. Lewis was used to Dad having a go at him, and being talked about as if he was not actually there. Dad had been doing it since he was a small child. His other self, his old self, would have just sat down and tried to ignore him, wanting to cry, gulping the misery back down inside. Now Lewis sat down and returned the gloating look, stare for stare. His father dropped his glance first, concentrating on his plate, stabbing up another load of dinner. He carried the freighted fork to his mouth and chewed thoughtfully before saying,

'Either that – or there must be something wrong with her. Got to be.'

'What do you mean?' Despite his best intentions, Lewis could feel himself rising to the bait.

'I don't know,' his father shrugged, 'why won't other boys go out with her?'

'They will. They do . . .'

'If that's right,' his father grinned as he continued to chew, 'then what is she doing with you?'

He swallowed his mouthful of food and chuckled to himself, confident that he had scored some sort of victory.

'I'm leaving the table.' Lewis stood up. 'Excuse me.'

'But Lewis,' his mother looked up at him, her face creased with concern, 'you've hardly eaten a thing.'

Lewis pushed back his chair. 'Not hungry.'

'That's it!' his father jeered. 'Run away.'

'I am not running away,' Lewis said evenly, only a sudden flush of colour and a muscle jumping in his cheek betrayed the fury he felt underneath. 'I've got homework. It has to be in tomorrow morning.'

'What did I do?' his father said as Lewis left the room, walking out on them. 'I was only joking, only teasing him a bit. What's the harm in that?'

'It didn't sound like joking,' his mother replied dubiously.

'Cuh! That's the trouble with you two: take everything too seriously. When I was a lad his age, my dad used to take the mickey out of me something chronic. You mollycoddle him, Lil. Always have, always will. Turned him into a right little la-d-di-da Little Lord Fauntleroy. With his fancy clothes, and fancy food, and fancy this and that. That's what's wrong with that boy. He needs to toughen up.'

★

A fantasy flashed up on a screen inside Lewis's head. A scene in which he grabbed his father round the neck, wrestled him to the ground and slowly squeezed the life out of him. He could possibly do it, too. He was bigger, taller and probably stronger. But violence was not the answer to anything. Mr Ladslow had taught him that. Violent emotions were always destructive, filling the body with poisonous toxins. He had taught Lewis to resist rather than attack; instructing him to build a brick wall in his mind, proof against any assault. Lewis went to his room. Not to do his homework but to practise his yoga.

His bedroom was sparsely furnished, spotlessly clean, and very tidy. Lewis had attended to this himself, putting a fresh coat of paint on the walls, throwing out everything that was not absolutely necessary. He had made a special area in the corner by the window. It was like a little shrine. A mat was set out in front of a low table which held candles, a variety of different kinds of crystals, a vase of fresh flowers and an incense holder. This was where he settled himself to meditate.

At first, he had felt self-conscious, silly even, and had found it hard to discipline his mind, to clear all the flying thoughts out of his head, but he was past that stage now. He quickly put himself into a light trance, staring fixedly into the soft oval brightness of light from a single candle, seeing nothing. Thoughts, pictures, memories entered his mind one at a time to be examined, evaluated and dismissed, until only one remained. The image came back again and again, so Lewis finally let it be. It was a face: milk white and thin, with fine sculpted features, a narrow bridged nose, high cheekbones, pointed chin. It was the face of a replicate, and should have been blank, expressionless, but yet it held a look of infinite sadness.

11

Dr McAllister looked down at the body in the bed. He stepped round, checked on the tubes snaking in and out of the thin pale form, bringing in nutrients, removing waste. The only sound was the rhythmic suck of the breathing machine and the regular bleep of the monitors, there to measure the level of activity, such as it was, keep a check on the vital functions. McAllister checked on these too, more for something to do than in the likelihood of any change being registered.

He turned from the machines to the other human presence in the room.

'Any signs?' he asked the nurse in the corner.

She shook her head, no. McAllister sighed, not that he'd been expecting it, but you never knew with coma cases. He went closer now, right up to the bed, and bent over the inert form, his white coat falling open, forming a kind of curtain. He held back the eyelids, one at a time, shining a pencil light into the blue eyes. Nothing. No reaction. The pupils remained at the same aperture. Little circles of blackness. What did they say? 'The eyes are the windows into the soul.' Something like that. The doctor flicked off the torch, letting the lids descend. There was nothing there.

He looked down at the boy. This patient was a puzzle, a profound mystery. To the police. To everybody. In repose like this, he just looked asleep. He had been suffering from mild hypothermia when they brought him in, but that was all. There was no trauma to the head, no wounding, no bruising. Hair, baby fine and fair, was growing back to cover his shaved scalp. The body was a little thin, but certainly not emaciated. There were no signs of any physical injuries there, either. He had no track marks on his arms, or anywhere else, all the drug tests had come up negative. No traces of any substances, legal or illegal, in his blood stream. He had been X-rayed, brain scanned, body scanned, ECGed, and all the tests they did came up with nothing. Metabolic rates were normal. There was no medical reason to explain why this patient should be in this state next to death with machines doing the living for him.

The nurse had come over now to stand beside the bed.

'Are you going to, you know . . .' her eyes indicated the battery of machines.

McAllister finished the question for her.

'Turn him off? We don't even know who he is . . .'

He frowned. To him, that seemed worse than anything else. He was a neurologist and had treated comatose patients before. Usually there were relatives, friends, care and concern thronging round the bed; but this young man had nothing, not even a name. The nurses had started calling him Brad after one of them had fancied a resemblance to an American film star. That was something he supposed.

'I read a thing in the paper,' the nurse volunteered, 'there have been other cases, haven't there?'

McAllister nodded. 'Several, apparently. That copper who's been in, what's his name? – Sutherland – he said that the police are only just now beginning to make the connection, and there's almost nothing to go on. They were all found on big city sites in different parts of the country. All stripped and shaven, with no identifying signs on any of them, clean of all forensic evidence, even down to their fingernails. No clues as to how they got there. No clear motive. No signs of assault, for example. Apart from the way the bodies are presented, the deaths could be put down to natural causes.'

'Someone must know who they are. I mean, wouldn't they be reported missing?'

'Depends.' McAllister shrugged, arms folded. 'They could be street kids, itinerants. More than a quarter of a million people go missing every year,' he nodded towards the bed, 'more than half of those are youngsters like him. Police resources are stretched to the limit.' He shook his head. 'I don't hold out much hope of them being able to identify him, to be honest. Not unless he comes round and tells us himself.'

'That'd take a miracle.'

'Yes. There's always that.'

'Always what?'

'Always a miracle.'

McAllister stared down at the boy, at his flawless beauty, his changeless state. Suddenly he bent forward. There was something on his face. He touched the cheek, and his finger came back wet. He put it to his mouth and tasted salt. An irritation? Dust under the lids? An allergic reaction to something in the atmosphere? Could be any of those, or somehow, somewhere deep in the lost confines of his comatose mind, this boy had been crying.

12

Lewis did not tell Jennie about the replicate that looked like the boy in the shop. Partly because by mid week he had more or less convinced himself that the whole thing was perfectly innocent. OK, making a doll of someone you knew might seem a bit odd, but not if you make a living out of manufacturing models, like Ladslow did, but it would be impossible to explain that to Jennie. She didn't trust Ladslow and she'd think the whole thing was weird. She'd tell Lewis to give up the job and he could not afford to, not yet. There was still her present to get. Also there was another reason he was finding it hard to talk to her at the moment, something that had nothing to do with toy shops or Viktor Ladslow.

'What's the matter?' Jennie asked, and for the second time received no reply.

Lewis was walking her home after school, but she might as well have been on her own for all the attention he was giving her. Jennie was beginning to wish now that she had gone on the bus with Carrie.

'I said,' she took hold of his bicycle handlebars, bringing him to a forcible halt, 'what is the matter?'

'Nothing.'

Lewis went to go on, but Jennie would not let go of his bike.

'Don't give me that. You've been "off" with me all day. It's been like you're avoiding me. Now you're acting like I'm not here.' She looked up at him, her expression mixed annoyance and concern. 'What's wrong, Lewis?'

'I told you,' he tugged the bike out of her grip. 'Nothing.'

'Fine.' Jennie took a step away from him, arms folded, her eyes clouding green with anger now. 'If you're in such a hurry to go, don't let me stop you.'

'I'm not in a hurry to go.'

'Well, you don't want to be with me, you've made that quite clear.'

'I do, honestly. It's just . . .'

'Just what?'

Lewis stood straddling his bike, staring down at the ground under the front wheel.

'It's just, I think maybe,' his voice tailed off, 'you don't want to be with me.'

'Oh?' Jennie moved a bit closer. 'And why should you think that?'

'It was something Dad said, and then, and then, lunchtime,' he paused, 'I saw you talking to Ross . . .'

'And that's all?'

'Yes, but . . .' Lewis picked at the rubber webbing on the handle grips. 'Maybe that's enough.'

'What did your dad say exactly?'

'He said,' Lewis sighed, 'he said, he couldn't understand what a girl like you was doing with someone like me. He said you'd dump me.'

'Oh, I see. And your dad can see inside my head, is that right? He knows, after one meeting, exactly what sort of person I am?'

'No. But he knows what sort of person I am.'

Jennie was standing in front of him now. She put out her gloved hands to cover his. 'No, he doesn't, Lewis.'

'What about Ross?' Lewis did not look up.

'What about him? Carrie said he wanted to see me. That he had some stuff to give me. Stuff I'd left round at his house. We were together a long time, I could hardly say no . . .'

'And what happened?'

'We met. He gave me the stuff. That's it.'

'Really?'

'Yes, really. Well, almost,' Jennie paused for a moment, and then went on. 'He wanted me to go back with him. He said he missed me, couldn't live without me, said we were so right for each other – you know the kind of thing.'

Lewis didn't, but he nodded anyway. 'What else?' he asked huskily. 'What else did he say?'

'He said he loved me, if you must know,' Jennie laughed a little shakily, 'not that he understands what it means.

He went on and on, wouldn't take no for an answer.' She frowned. 'He really seems to think he's got a chance. I don't know where he got that idea, maybe Carrie's been encouraging him . . .'

'What did you say?'

'I said, "No", and I meant it. I'm not going back with him.' Jennie reached up and pushed his dark red fringe away so she could see into his eyes. 'You've got to trust me, Lewis.'

'I know, it's just . . .'

'Just what?'

'Sometimes it seems like Dad has got a point.' He laughed humourlessly, turning away from her. 'What on earth does a girl like you see in a guy like me?'

'Look. Look at me.' Jennie pulled him round to face her. 'You are one of the nicest people I've ever met, certainly the nicest boy . . .' she grinned up at him, touching him on the chin with her gloved fist. 'Besides that you're gorgeous.'

'What me? Don't be stupid!'

'You are, you know,' Jennie laughed. 'I'm going to be fighting 'em off you soon.' She shook her head. 'I don't know how you did it, but you've gone from fat boy to hunk in about a month. I was just the first to notice, now the rest of them are on the case.'

'How do you know?'

'Oh, come on! It's a good thing *I'm* not the jealous type!'

'What do you mean?' Lewis looked down at her, curious.

'OK.' Jennie began marking them off on her fingers. 'Josie Peters was chatting you up this morning before school, Angie Smith in French, Sandy Lawrence at break, plus half the netball team at lunch . . .'

'Hey, hey, wait.' Lewis put up his hands in protest. 'Josie was asking me if I'd help with the school paper, do the layout. Angie wanted to know if I'd be interested in joining the swimming club because she saw me down the baths last week.'

Jennie's eyebrows rose, 'I bet she did.'

'And as for the netball team,' Lewis shrugged, 'they are just in the gym . . .'

'Is that right?' Jennie's mouth twisted in an ironic grin. 'Perfecting their passing? Getting in a little shooting practice? They are there to check on the guys working out. Everyone knows that.' She laughed at the look on his face. 'Everyone except you. That's what I love about you . . .'

'Just that?' Lewis smiled back.

'Among other things.' She shook his arm. 'Now, come on, Lewis. You've been doing brilliantly. Don't blow it now. Keep on believing in yourself.'

'I do . . . It's just hard, with Dad banging on all the time. Having you on my side helps, though. I don't know what I'd do if . . .'

She reached up, putting a finger on his lips to stop his words.

'Hey, shh. What did I just say? I'm not letting Josie and Angie and that lot think they are in with a chance. There's no way that's going to happen. Now,' she linked arms with him as they walked along. 'Do you want to come back to my place?' She smiled, her blue green eyes teasing and bright. 'My folks are going out tonight and I really could do with some help with my Maths homework.'

13

By the end of the week, Lewis was feeling much better about everything. So much better that he had consented to take Jennie to a party on Friday night. Someone's 18th. He went under protest, thinking he would hate it: he didn't know the people, he wasn't exactly a party animal, but he had really enjoyed himself. All of a sudden, he was popular! It was like magic! He was with the prettiest girl there, everyone wanted to be his friend. But having a great time can have a downside. He'd overslept and woken with an aching head and this made him late for work.

'Ah, Lewis!' Viktor Ladslow came to open the door. 'I thought you weren't going to make it. I thought you might be sick . . .'

'Yeah.' Lewis took off his coat. 'Sorry I'm late today. I had a problem getting up.'

'Late night?'

'Something like that.'

'Good time?'

'A bit too much of a good time.' Lewis gave a rueful

grin. 'We went to a party. I've got a bit of a headache, to be honest. I guess I'm not used to it.'

'Come through to the back.' Viktor Ladslow was all concern. 'I've got just the thing for that. A little remedy that will cure it in no time.' He busied himself, opening a sachet, dropping the contents into a glass. 'Here, knock it back. You said, *we* went to a party,' he added, conversationally, 'are you still going out with Jennie?'

'Oh, yes.' Lewis swallowed the potion and smiled. 'Very much so.'

'Good.' Viktor Ladslow smiled back, warmed by the transforming look on the boy's face. 'That's excellent. A lovely girl that. You are lucky. How are you feeling? Better?'

Lewis looked down at the glass in his hand. 'Yes, thanks. This stuff's magic.'

'Just a little concoction I made up myself. Remind me to give you a couple of sachets. Now,' he rubbed his hands, 'you go and flip over the "Open" sign. It's time to meet the public, Lewis.'

Lewis did not have much opportunity to think about Jennie, or anything else for the rest of the day. There was only one more Saturday to go before Christmas, and the shop was packed. What with serving, and keeping an eye out for shoplifters, Lewis was kept very busy. He and Mr Ladslow both manned the counter, the tarot readings were on hold at the moment; that part of the business could wait until the New Year when trade slackened off a bit. Lewis did not even have a break until late afternoon when the crowds began to ebb and Ladslow judged that the main rush was over.

'Why don't you put the kettle on,' he said, 'and have a sit down. I'll mind the shop.'

'Are you sure?'

Ladslow waved him away. 'Of course. Bring my tea out to me and then go and put your feet up for a bit.'

'OK.'

'While you're out there, can you bring some more stock in? We're running low on those spaceman action figures and the Vacation Barbies.'

'Do you want them now?'

'No, no,' Ladslow shook his head. 'Take a break first. You can do that afterwards.'

Lewis went through to the kitchen. He was not saying 'No'. What with being out until late last night, and the kind of day he'd been having here, he was feeling pretty shattered.

He took Ladslow his tea and then went back to have his break. He'd thought about having another look in the Finishing Room, but it remained that, just a thought, until he went to the Stock Room. The door was right next to it. He could always say he got confused. It would not hurt to take a look. Just one. Just to make certain . . .

He tried the handle. The door was open.

Lewis put his head round cautiously, not quite sure what he expected to find. Whatever it was, he was destined to be disappointed. The room was empty. There was no replicate lodged against the wall. There was nothing at all: the tools put away, the machines, turned off. All he could see were a few bolts of cloth. Whatever had been in there had been shipped off. Lewis sighed with relief and withdrew hastily, closing the door. He did not want to be caught spying. Ladslow had obviously cleared the decks for another project.

Lewis returned to the shop carrying the boxes Ladslow had ordered.

'Find what you wanted?' the man asked.

'What?'

'The toys. Were they easy to find? Stock Room's got in a bit of a mess again, I'm afraid. I haven't had a chance to tidy up properly.'

Lewis put the boxes down and began arranging the toys on the shelves.

'I can give you a hand tomorrow, if you like,' he said. 'Sort the Stock Room out for you.'

'No. That will not be possible.' Ladslow stroked his silky beard. 'I have a client coming. All the way from Switzerland. I have a very special project I am hoping to interest him in.'

'Do you think you might have sold them?'

'Sold what?' A look of caution stole across Ladslow's face.

'That line of toys you've been developing.'

'Yes,' Ladslow's face cleared and his hand strayed to his chin again as he smiled. 'That's exactly it. Tomorrow I hope to swing the deal.'

'You won't be needing me, then?'

'No, your presence will not be necessary. You can catch up on all that school work, spend some time with your family.' He laughed at Lewis's grimace. 'Like that, is it?'

'Just a bit,' Lewis grinned.

'Perhaps you can take Jennie somewhere?'

'She has homework of her own to do and her folks to keep company.'

'Never mind,' Ladslow smiled. 'Are you meeting her tonight?'

'Yeah. From work.' Lewis looked at his watch and then at the clock. His watch had stopped. 'Is that the time?' It was pitch dark outside. He hadn't noticed. 'I'm late—'

'Don't panic. She'll wait. Here,' Ladslow opened the till and counted out Lewis's wages. 'And have this.' He put an extra ten pound note in. 'Take her somewhere nice.'

'Yes, I will. Thanks, Mr Ladslow.'

Lewis stuffed the money into his trouser pocket. As he did so, the door tinged behind him and Jennie walked into the shop.

'Where have you been? I thought you were going to get away early. I've been waiting ages.'

'I'm really sorry.' Lewis held up his wrist. 'My watch stopped and I didn't notice. We were rushed off our feet earlier—'

'Never mind. Can't be helped, I suppose.' Her scowl turned to a smile at the contrite look on his face. She was just about to kiss him when she saw the toy shop owner lurking behind the counter. 'Oh, hello, Mr Ladslow.'

'Hello Jennie, my dear. Might I say how charming you look tonight?'

'Oh,' Jennie looked down at herself. Her coat was open, showing off her new jeans and lilac coloured top. She'd bought them today at discount and changed before she left the shop. 'Thank you.'

'That colour goes so well with your eyes. Brings out the blue rather than the green . . .' He stroked his moustache, his eyes travelling over her slowly, taking in every detail. Jennie tried to keep her smile, but she was suppressing a shudder. It was almost as if he was touching her. 'What do you think, Lewis?'

'Umm, yes,' Lewis glanced over towards his girlfriend, 'very nice.'

Ladslow let out a sharp laugh. 'You hadn't even noticed! You must pay attention to such things. It doesn't do to take such a lovely young lady for granted.'

Lewis moved towards Jennie, an instinctive, protective gesture.

'That's better!' His smile now included both of them. 'My, you do look handsome together!' His black eyes crinkled at the sides and beamed, taking on an almost proprietorial gleam, then his manner changed. 'Well, I mustn't keep you,' he said, rubbing his hands, brisk and businesslike. 'Off you go. You have a good time together.'

'We will,' they said and left the shop, arms round each other. 'Thanks, Mr Ladslow.'

'Thank you,' Ladslow said to himself as he turned the notice on the door to 'Closed'.

Having activated the alarm, he went into the back of the shop, leaving just the security lights on. There he made a brew of his special tea, Darjeeling First Flush, and took it in his china mug through to the Finishing Room. He went over to the shelf and took down the bolts of cloth, caressing the different fabrics. Crisp check cotton and velvet ribbed cord for the boy; soft denim and silk jersey for the girl, just the right shade of pale violet, a particularly fine choice, even if he said so himself.

He cut and shaped, pins frilling his mouth. Young love. First love. It only happened once. It would never be the same again. It was a richness beyond price. If only you could package and sell it. If only you could. Viktor Ladslow began to sew.

14

'So what if he does hear,' Lewis was shouting now. 'I don't care. He's got a real nerve, having a go at me . . .'

'You were rather late,' his mother looked up at him, eyes pleading, trying to stop another argument. 'And it was two nights in a row.'

'Oh, yeah? Is that so? And what time does he normally crawl in?'

'He can crawl in any time he likes,' his father emerged from the bathroom, in pyjama bottoms and vest, wiping shaving foam from his face. 'Because *he's* the man of the house. He's not sixteen and staying out to all hours with some young tart.'

'She's not a tart!'

'Is that right?' his father laughed, cleaning out his ears with a corner of the towel. 'That's not what I heard.'

'You don't know what you're talking about!' Lewis shook his head. 'You're just saying that!'

'Am I now? That's all you know.' The grin widened. 'Does the name Ross Horton ring a bell?'

'Yes,' Lewis muttered, 'he goes to our school. So what?'

'He was down the club last evening, with his brother and some lads from the soccer team, having a drink after the match. From what he was saying, sounded like he'd been there, along with most of the rest of the Saturday League. Told you there was something wrong with her, didn't I? Used goods.'

'You're lying!'

'Am I? Am I, though? Why don't you come down and ask them? Come on. Come with me now. They'll soon tell you – she's a real—'

'I could kill you!' Unable to bear any more, Lewis lunged towards his father. 'I could kill you!'

'Oh, yeah? You and whose army?' His father mimed fear, dodging back as Lewis came forward. 'I'm so scared.'

'Lewis, don't!' His mother grabbed hold of him, pulling him back. He tore himself away from her and ran down the stairs. 'Where are you going?'

'Out!'

'Let him go, Lil. He'll be back. Needs to grow up, that lad. Learn to take the truth.'

'It's not the truth and you know it! Why can't you just leave him alone!'

Lillian James burst into tears and ran into the bathroom. Her husband could hear her sobbing through the door. He went into the bedroom to get dressed. It got more like a soap opera here every day. He smoothed his hair down and put on his watch. Midday. Time for a pint. What he needed to do was get down the club double quick, have himself a drink and get into some real company.

Lewis ran and ran until he couldn't run any more. He had left the house without a coat and it was bitterly cold. His breath plumed in the air as he walked along, wandering the deserted town. It was early afternoon, his mother would be serving lunch soon, but he was not going back. He'd rather freeze in the streets, he'd rather starve than spend another minute under the same roof as that bastard. He would leave. Now. Hitchhike out. Head for London or somewhere and never come back. But if he did that, he'd never see Jennie again. Her folks were not the kind to let her associate with a street itinerant. Maybe she could go with him. They could strike off, find a new life somewhere else, be together, forever. He shook his head as he walked along. That was a stupid idea, Lewis thought as he sat in the park; but it was a dream that kept the cold at bay – for some of the time, anyway.

There was some kind of pre-Christmas fair in the Market Square so he wandered round that until the stallkeepers were packing up and it was growing dark. It had been a fine day but dusk comes early in December. He knew that he would have to go home soon, but he was putting it off until the very last minute. The coffee bar on the corner was open. It was light and bright and warm in there. Lewis dug in his pocket, seeing if he had enough cash on him for a cup of something.

He settled in the corner, wrapping his frozen hands round his mug. Now he was inside he could not stop shivering. He wiped a space in the condensation and glanced out into the darkening square. There was a big car, looked like a limo, parked in the side street down by Ladslow's. Lewis cleared a bigger space to get a better look. The car must belong to Ladslow's big-shot client.

The woman in the café was wanting to close up. Lewis sipped his tea slowly, reluctant to go out into the freezing cold, but one by one the other customers left and the proprietor went round wiping tables and stacking chairs behind them. Eventually she came over to where Lewis was sitting and gave the formica a big blast of Mr Muscle, a fine mist of spray landing on what was left of his tea. Lewis judged that it was time to make a move.

He checked out the car on his way past. The big Mercedes had foreign plates. The bumper sticker said 'CH'. This guy must have driven all the way from Switzerland. He must be very keen to get hold of whatever Ladslow had to offer. Through the smoked glass, Lewis could see the outline of the chauffeur, sitting in the front seat, still as stone.

He walked along slowly, trying to look casual, not wanting the guy to think he was spying. Then the side door of the shop opened and Ladslow came out. He had a jacket on, which was unusual for him, generally he went around in shirt sleeves. Lewis dodged into the entrance to the alley almost directly opposite, curious to know what was going on, but not wanting to be seen by the two men. Ladslow's friend was much shorter, he only came up to the toy shop owner's shoulder, but he was powerfully built. He had a little goatee beard and an expensive overcoat, one of those fancy kinds with a curly fur collar. His narrow brimmed hat was pulled down, shading a not very pleasant face, pouchy-eyed, pale-skinned and pudgy.

'If it is how you say it is,' he was saying, 'it will be very satisfactory, very satisfactory indeed. In the past there has been certain,' he paused, 'malfunctioning, which is always distressing, and we are talking about a very large sum of money.'

'Don't worry yourself on that score,' Ladslow assured him. 'This will be the best yet.' He put his hand on the man's shoulder, guiding him towards the door the chauffeur had opened. 'The most sophisticated entertainment the world has yet seen, for your use exclusively. It will be worth every centime. It will be my masterpiece.'

'When can you deliver?'

'Christmas. There will be fine tuning and a certain amount of tidying up to do here and then I will bring it over personally. Set it up for you and stay to attend to any teething troubles which might occur.'

'Very well.' The man nodded as if satisfied. He extended a gloved hand and Ladslow shook it. 'If the outcome is pleasing, the rest of the money will be in your account by the New Year.'

The heavy door thunked shut and the chauffeur returned

to the driver's seat. The huge car pulled away with hardly a whisper from the powerful engine, leaving Ladslow alone in the street, smiling to himself.

Lewis pulled further back into the shadows. The alley behind him led to a dead end. Despite the cold, which was really biting now, he would have to wait until Ladslow had gone. He did not want the toy shop owner to think that he had been watching and curiosity had made him stay too long. It was not just that, the look on Ladslow's face, the gloating grin which remained long after the car had disappeared, made him even more reluctant to show himself.

Lewis might have wanted to avoid Ladslow, but Ladslow saw him all right. He'd seen him earlier from his upstairs window and wondered what the boy was doing wandering about without a coat in mid December. You did not have to be a genius to work out the reason, and Viktor Ladslow's insight was extremely acute. Trouble at home. Trouble enough to send him out on to the streets. It couldn't be more perfect.

He had also glimpsed the boy dodging into the alley opposite the shop. Breath shows like smoke on a night as cold as this. He knew that the boy had lingered. That was a little worrying. Ladslow went back over his conversation with Monsieur LeBlanc. Could the boy have overheard anything of importance? He quickly dismissed any fears on that score. He would understand nothing of what they were saying. He would not be able to guess, not in a million years, at the fate Viktor Ladslow had in store for him. Even if he did, by some immense feat of deductive reasoning, by some enormous leap of the imagination, it would not matter. Events were in train. By this time next week the project would be complete and there was nothing, absolutely nothing that he could do about it.

The boy had had his fun. Ladslow had granted him every wish he'd ever wanted. And, after all, a bargain is a bargain.

A deal is a deal.

15

The Saturday before Christmas. One of the busiest trading days of the year. Cars were pouring into the town. Lewis wove his bike in and out and down the lines of traffic stopped at the lights, or queuing up to get into the car parks or the multi-storey. The centre was filling up. The pavement outside Toys'N'Gifts was already thronged with people intent on making an early start, getting their shopping over and done with.

If Lewis had thought last week was busy, it was nothing compared with this. Customers were gathered outside, ready to surge in as soon as Ladslow flipped the sign to 'Open'. Lewis knew why. Ladslow had kept back a large supply of the season's most popular toy, the one that all the kids wanted. Every other shop had run out. Ladslow had the only stock left for miles about. There they were, piled up in the window. Parents would be fighting over them, desperate to keep Christmas morning disappointment away from their house. If they came into the shop for that one thing, and got it, they'd buy other stuff out of sheer relief. If they could not get what they wanted, they'd buy something else, probably more expensive. Folks were getting desperate now, no-one would risk leaving the shop empty-handed. Lewis had to hand it to him, Mr Ladslow was a very smart businessman.

Apart from big, expensive items the shop did a brisk trade in stocking fillers and smaller presents. Girls came in droves to paw through the jewellery and crystals and aromatherapy stuff, buying New Age junk for their friends, scented candles for their mums. Children dug out piles of change to pay for pocket money toys for their mates or little brothers and sisters.

Lewis didn't mind. Being busy was a good thing. It kept his mind off other things. The atmosphere at home for a start. He had arrived home on Sunday to find his mum just about to phone the police. Even his dad had looked worried. He had torn into Lewis, screaming at him about the trouble he caused, the worry he gave his mother. Lewis had lost it, too. Shouting back that he was not a little kid any more, he was nearly an adult, with a right to freedom and privacy. Neither of them cared about or respected that, which meant they didn't really care about him as a person. They would probably be better off without him. None of it was true, of course. But you don't think about that in the middle of a row, do you?

Things had got worse since then. No healing words had been uttered between him and his father. There had been no reconciliation. If he walked into a room, his dad walked out, and vice versa. His mother spent most of the time in tears, caught between the two of them. Lewis hated to see her upset like this and, as Dad wouldn't do anything, he felt as if it was all up to him. So far he had failed to come up with any answers and could see no clear route to reconciliation.

Mum had suggested Sunday lunch out, a family day together, she'd asked Lewis what he thought. He didn't hold out too many hopes, but had promised to keep the day free and to be on his best behaviour. He would make the effort, for her sake. Tell Ladslow he wouldn't be available this Sunday, try and be nice to Dad, talk to him about his work, or cars, or sport, things he was interested in. Perhaps that would do the trick.

'Are you all right, Lewis?' Mr Ladslow asked in one of the rare lulls during the morning. 'It's just you seem rather troubled. Not your usual sunny self.'

'No. I'm fine,' Lewis replied, aware that his subdued behaviour had probably betrayed something of the turmoil going on inside him.

'Trouble at home again?' Ladslow guessed.

'Well, in a way.'

'Anything I can do?'

'Yes. I was going to ask if . . .'

Lewis had no time to finish what he was about to say. A father and son arrived in front of him. The small boy dumped a pile of toys and stickers and carefully counted coins he held in his fist. His dad helped him, smiling, and then ruffled the lad's hair before reaching into his pocket to make up the shortfall. Viktor Ladslow left Lewis to serve them and turned with a ready smile to help an old lady choose a toy for her grandson. There was no need to confirm the source of Lewis's unhappiness. He could read it, plainer than words, clearly written on the boy's face.

The rest of the day was hectic. Lewis had to go without a break again, and he had no time to speak to Mr Ladslow until about half-past four. Suddenly the shop cleared. It was as if some kind of signal called all the customers away again. The shop was deserted. Lewis looked out from behind the counter. Half the shelves were empty. Displays had been toppled. Boxes and sets lay strewn about from where they had been moved and not put back.

'It often happens like that,' Mr Ladslow commented. 'It will be the same on Christmas Eve. The place is packed, then suddenly it's all over. It's as though they exhaust themselves.' He surveyed the chaos spread around him. 'Perhaps you can come in tomorrow to help me tidy up and re-stock?'

'Er, well,' Lewis was embarrassed. 'I was going to talk to you about that. I can't. Not tomorrow.'

'Why not?' A dark look stole like a shadow over Ladslow's face. 'I was counting on you . . .'

'We're going out to lunch – as a family – Mum's arranging it specially . . .'

'Oh, Lewis, you disappoint me. I was counting on you . . .'

Lewis shook his head. 'I just can't. Sorry.'

The boy's mouth was setting in a stubborn line, his tone of voice decisive, making it clear that he had made up his mind and was not to be dissuaded. Ladslow sighed. He had been relying on Lewis being there this Sunday and had been about to invite the girl too, for a little pre-Christmas celebration. He did not like his plans thwarted, but he would not insist. He did not want to alert the boy. He would just have to improvise something, find some other means of luring him in.

He was just about to say something when the shop door tinged, announcing another customer. It was Carrie, Jennie's best friend.

'Hi, Lewis,' she said, flicking her curly black hair back from her face. She smiled but it was a strain. Lewis could see in her eyes that she still did not like him. 'How'ya doing?'

'OK.'

Carrie nodded. 'Got a message from Jen. She wants to know if you can meet her.'

'When? Now?'

'Yeah. She's getting off early to do some shopping. Wants you to go with her.'

'Well, it's not up to me . . .' Lewis turned to Viktor Ladslow.

'Go,' the shop owner shrugged. 'Like I said, the main rush is over. There won't be that many coming in at this time. I can cope on my own now.'

'If you're certain . . .'

114

'Yes. I'll be perfectly OK.'

'Just get my coat, then,' Lewis said to Carrie.

'Sure. Fine.' Carrie shifted uneasily, the shop was empty and she felt the same way about Ladslow as Jennie did. She moved towards the door. 'I'll wait for you outside.'

'Lewis?' Ladslow called him back. 'Haven't you forgotten something?'

'What?'

'Your money. The only thing is . . .' Ladslow patted his pocket. 'I can't give it to you yet. I'm a bit short of readies and I don't really want to take it out of the register until I've cashed up . . . and I was going to give you a little bit extra – call it a Christmas bonus.' He appeared to think for a while. 'As you are going to be in town, perhaps you could call back later? You and Jennie? Perhaps the two of you would like to join me in a pre-Christmas drink?'

'Sure.' Lewis shrugged. 'Be glad to.' Carrie was waving through the window, beckoning for him to hurry up. 'See you later, Mr Ladslow.'

The shopkeeper saw the boy out and watched him join Carrie who was already crossing the road. He waited a minute or so, until they were out of sight, and then he turned the sign to 'Closed'. Anyone wishing to make a late purchase was in for a disappointment. Mr Ladslow had to attend to other business.

16

The others shops were still open, spilling light and piped carols onto pavements crowded with shoppers, Big Issue sellers, street vendors selling cheap wrapping paper. Lewis followed Carrie through the throng. Above their heads the town's Christmas lights spangled and shone, suspended against the black sky like jewelled bracelets. Carrie walked on. She was leading Lewis away from the centre to a different area altogether.

'Where are we going?'

'Shh,' Carrie put a finger to her lips. He could not read her eyes and her smile looked sly in the orange street light. 'You'll see. It's a surprise.'

They appeared to be going towards the station. Lewis stuffed his hands in his coat pockets and pulled up his collar. It was another bitter night. He really had no idea why Jennie would want to meet him there, but she had sent Carrie, so there must be some reason behind it.

'We'll go this way.' Carrie cut down an alley that led to

a footpath which followed the line of the railway track. 'It's a short cut.'

'Hold up a minute, Carrie.' Lewis caught her arm. 'Where are you taking me?'

'I told you. Wait and see. It's a secret.'

'Hang on!' he called, but she was off again.

Lewis followed, but reluctantly. It was dark down here. Most of the street lights were out, broken or vandalised. The path they were heading for was deserted, not much frequented. Maybe Jennie was playing some kind of game with him. He shook his head, dismissing the possibility. She wouldn't do that, she was not that kind of girl. Carrie, though. Carrie was different. He looked at the diminutive figure walking in front of him, hunched up in her puffer jacket. She didn't like Lewis and she could be very vindictive . . .

He was just about to turn back, convinced that this was a waste of time, when Carrie stopped. They were on the railway footpath now. Scrub and brambles straggled away on one side and on the other chainlink fencing separated the path from the line which ran below them at the bottom of a steep embankment. Carrie had stopped where a road bridge crossed both path and track. The rusting, riveted parapet was scrawled with graffiti. Jennie would never have arranged to meet him here. This had to be a wind-up.

He was just about to ask Carrie what was going on, when she was joined by someone else. Not Jennie. The figure was unmistakably male.

'Hello, Lewis,' Ross Horton grinned at him, hands in pockets. 'Surprise, surprise.'

Ross must have been waiting under the bridge. He was coming towards him now, walking wide-legged, shoulders forward, hands balled into fists. Lewis backed up, his own hands held palm out in a gesture of peace.

'I don't know why you brought me here, but I don't want to fight you, man.'

'Who says you're gonna have a choice? I told you,' Ross was in his face now, 'keep away from her!' He dragged the words out, shouting up at Lewis, spraying his chin with spit.

'Isn't it up to her to decide?' Lewis asked, keeping his voice mild.

'No!' Ross shouted, eyes slitted, teeth bared. 'She's mine! You got a lesson coming, fat boy. One you will not forget!'

Lewis stared down at the other boy, squaring up to him. He didn't want to fight, but if he had to, he would. Ross had a reputation, he was known for being something of a psycho, but that did not scare Lewis. He breathed deeply, in through his nose, out through his mouth, adjusting his balance, curling his hands into fists.

A high-pitched giggle, half smothered, came from under the bridge where Carrie must be watching. The peculiar tone, skittering along the edge of hysteria, alerted Lewis a fraction too late.

He heard footsteps coming up behind him. Ross was not here on his own, he had reinforcements. Sounded like there were two of them. Probably Mick and Paul, Ross's mates. Lewis knew them and thought he could take them too, in a fair fight. But this was not going to be a fair fight. Before he could turn round, he was grabbed from behind by unseen hands, his half open coat dragged down from his shoulders. Someone big was breathing in his ear, someone taller than him, too tall to be Mick or Paul. It must be Ross's older brother with one of his friends. Lewis could not turn his head to see, but he didn't need to, he knew. These were men, not other boys like him. He was in for a beating.

He struggled, but his arms were held by his own coat, tight to his sides, as though he were in a straitjacket. Ross's mouth contorted into some kind of smile as he delivered the first of his punches, hitting Lewis in the solar plexus. Lewis doubled over. Hands gripped his hair, pulling his head up so Ross could aim another blow, hitting him on the chin this time. Lewis felt the sovereign ring Ross wore bite savagely into his jaw as his teeth clashed together. His head snapped back and the blackness above him exploded into stars and then became black again.

The arms holding him let go. Lewis slumped to his knees, thinking it was all over, when a kick sent him keeling over sideways on to the ground. He rolled up in a ball, as he'd seen other kids do at school, trying to protect himself as kicks dug into his back and ribs. A foot connected with the side of his head, setting off another firework burst of light. Lewis lay sprawled out, unable to even protect himself, as the darkness surged back for a second time.

Ross and his brother dragged Lewis to a gap in the wire and tipped him down the embankment. Ross listened, his body trembling, jittering with adrenalin. He laughed, high and triumphant, punching the air, shouting 'Yess!', as the heavy form crashed away through the undergrowth and brambles.

'Cold night,' his brother's mate observed as he zipped up his jacket.

'What if no-one finds him?' Carrie asked, staring down into the blackness.

She'd stayed under the parapet to watch, but came out once it was over.

'Exactly.' Ross laughed again, loud and harsh. He sucked his bruised knuckles and then stuffed his hand in his pocket. 'That's the whole point, you stupid bitch.'

17

Jennie was waiting at the agreed time at their normal meeting place but there was absolutely no sign of Lewis. She checked her watch again, he was already twenty minutes late. She looked up and down the street. All the shops were closing, one by one their lights were going out, shutters coming down. The pavements were empty except for a litter of plastic bags and food containers whipped around by the biting wind. A piece of brightly coloured paper, covered in fat jolly Santas, whirled up and wrapped itself round her legs. Jenny kicked it away and pulled her coat to her. It really was freezing. The shop workers were leaving now, calling goodbye to each other. There was no point in standing here any more looking like an idiot. Lewis was so bad at time-keeping. It was the same last week. Jenny shrugged and hitched her bag onto her shoulder. If he couldn't get it together enough to come to her, she would just have to go and find him.

The lights were still on in Ladslow's shop. She approached the neon-lit window, hoping that Lewis was still there and hadn't already left to go looking for her. If he had, they could be hunting each other round the town for hours.

She noted with relief that the sign was turned to 'Open'. Ladslow must be hanging on right to the end of the day, hoping to catch the last of the shoppers. They had obviously had a very busy day. Lewis probably felt he had to stay to help close up. That was so like him. The bell tinged as she opened the door. Ladslow was hovering just inside, almost as though he was waiting for her, but there was no sign of Lewis.

'You look cold,' he said as she entered. 'Come in, come in, my dear. Are you looking for Lewis?'

Jennie nodded.

'He is in the back, waiting for you. I am just going to close up and then we can go through and join him.'

Ladslow turned the sign back to 'Closed' and bolted the door.

Lewis came round with a start and lay, still as an animal, as something rushed past his face at tremendous speed. Lights streaked above him, and a noise, high-pitched, terrifying, screamed in his ears. The back draught flattened his hair, plastering it onto his forehead, and then the train was gone. Silence surged back. Lewis tried to get up, but couldn't. He hurt all over. His legs didn't seem to work properly and his head felt like a football. He was lying by the railway line, about a metre or so from the track. He rolled back and away from it, chunks of gravel crunching under him, and lay in the stiff dusty grass staring up at the embankment. His lips were swollen, and he tasted salt. Hot coppery blood filled his mouth, but whether the cuts were inside or out, he did not know.

He struggled up into a sitting position and immediately vomited, retching and spitting a mix of blood and mucus onto the oily ground. His sides ached and he touched his face gingerly. It was puffy and hot, criss-crossed with raised welts where the brambles had torn into him on his way down. The backs of his hands showed similar slashes, some of them still oozing.

He was in a mess, a real mess, but he couldn't stay here. It was dangerous. Electricity fizzed and sparked in the overhead cables and there could be another train along at any second. He had to get away from here. Up to the top.

The way he'd come down was impossible. He must have surfed over the top of an impenetrable thicket of brambles. Crawling on his hands and knees, he came to the base of the bridge and grasped on to the rough solid brickwork. Slowly, painfully, he pulled himself upright, one foot at a time, hand over hand.

Next to the bridge, a dirt track led to the path where he had been attacked, above that was the road. Crude steps had been cut into the steepest part of the slope and Lewis sank to his knees again, hauling himself up as if he was on a ladder. His raw palms stung as the fine black grit got into his cuts, and it seemed to take a long time, but eventually he was at the top of the cutting. He emerged from a gap between the fence and the bridge parapet and stayed, crouched on his hands and knees, gathering his strength to crawl up the next path which led to the road way.

He had to get back. He had to find Jennie. That was all Lewis could think about. He rested for a while when he got to the top, hugging onto the end of the bridge, mustering the power to go on. Then he started off, making his way back to the centre of town. One of his assailants had kicked him in the thigh and he had fallen awkwardly on the same leg; this skewed his gait making him limp and lurch along the pavement like a drunk.

There were not many people about to stare and wonder at the state he was in and he got as far as the multi-storey car park without being noticed. He ducked into the toilets, thinking to clean himself up a bit, but even Lewis was not prepared for the face in the cracked foggy mirror. A blood-masked stranger stared back at him, one eye half-closed, black as a split plum, the other bloodshot, red-rimmed and desperate.

He turned the taps full on, damming the grimy basin with a wad of toilet paper. Pain shot up his arms, bringing him near to screaming point, dulling all his other aches and pains, as he immersed his torn hands, washing black grit from the gouges and scratches as best he could. He emptied the silty bloody water, filling the basin again to sluice his face. He bathed the skin, washing gently at the crusted dried cuts, trying not to start any fresh bleeding. Luckily, most of the damage was superficial scraping and grazing.

Not too bad, he thought, looking back in the mirror. The black eye was still there and would get worse before it got better. There was a lump the size of an egg just above his right temple, and this was shiny and tender. That whole side of his face was swollen and ached, but at least it was clean of blood. He splashed water up straight from the tap and dried his face on his shirt, beginning to feel almost human again.

He came out into the cold air, the freezing temperature contracting the skin on his stinging cheeks, clearing his head still further. He pushed himself off the wall and walked on, leaving his pain behind, only one thing on his mind now. He had to find Jennie.

18

Jennie was not at their appointed meeting place, it was much too late for that. She was not at the bus stop. Lewis peered through the lighted windows of Mcdonald's, she was not in there, and everywhere else was shut. She was not anywhere in the square. Lewis stopped at a phone booth and dug clumsily in his pocket, checking with his damaged hands for loose change for the phone. Maybe she'd gone home, or maybe Carrie had gone to meet her instead of him. He'd call Jennie's mum, taking care not to alarm her, and then he'd call her friend.

Jennie was not at home. Lewis squinted in the light from the street lamp, trying to read the torn and soiled phone directory with his good eye. Luckily Carrie's number was one of the ones spared by the vandals.

'Is that Carrie?' he asked, when a girl's voice answered. 'It's Lewis here. Lewis James. Don't hang up, or I swear, I'll . . .'

Lewis was not sure what threat he was about to utter, but Carrie sounded relieved to hear him, almost tearful.

'Yes, I'm all right,' Lewis interrupted her stammered enquiry, cutting off her stumbling efforts at excuse and apology. 'Is Jennie there? Is she with you?'

Lewis replaced the receiver and reclaimed what was left of his money. The reply was negative. Only one place left to look. Lewis went from the phone box, cutting diagonally across the deserted square, heading for the shop on the corner. The interior was dark, one single spot lit the window. Up above the neon sign winked on and off: Toys'N'Gifts.

'Lewis! What took you so long? We've been expecting you. Oh dear, oh dear,' Ladslow's face changed as he observed the boy's physical state, his expression converting to one of apparent concern. 'Have you been in some kind of accident? Is that what delayed you? We've had to start without you, I'm afraid,' he went on, without waiting for an answer. 'Jennie's already here, enjoying a pre-Christmas celebration. Come in, come in.'

Lewis followed Ladslow through the darkened shop, through the beaded curtain and under the low arch that led into the back part. He expected to be shown into Ladslow's living quarters; but the room was empty, fire out and no lights on.

'Jennie *is* here?' Lewis asked, stopping outside, staring at the darkened interior.

'Oh, yes,' Ladslow replied. 'She's been waiting for you. Not in there, though.' He beckoned Lewis on down the corridor, past the glass-fronted cabinets which contained the museum exhibits. 'You'll find her in the Finishing Room.'

The workshop was in darkness, the benches cleared. The door to the Finishing Room was closed, but a strip of light showed from underneath it. Ladslow used this to guide them down the long room.

'Please,' Ladslow held the door for Lewis, 'go in.'

Lewis stood for a moment, blinking, his eyes getting used to the sudden fluorescent-lit brightness; while behind him, the door closed and a key turned in the lock.

'There,' Ladslow said, slipping the key into his pocket. 'Now we can be private. There's your Jennie. I told you she was waiting for you. Doesn't she look lovely?'

Ladslow smiled, caressing his black silky beard. Lewis followed his dark-eyed gaze to one corner where Jennie was sprawled, half sitting, half lying against the wall. She could have been sleeping, except her limbs looked too loose, her body too open, too abandoned, and the angle of her head was wrong. She could have been . . .

Lewis shook off the paralysing shock of seeing her, the feeling that this was not really happening, and was across the room in seconds.

'She's not dead,' Ladslow said, and laughed as the boy felt for a pulse.

Lewis failed to hear him, he was focussing all his attention on Jennie. Her head had rolled sideways exposing her profile. Ladslow was right: every detail was beautiful. The delicate angle of her jaw above the white column of her neck, the curve of her lips, rose red against flawless skin, pale with a slight pink flush. The closed eyes, violet lidded, under eyebrows arched and perfect, long lashes resting like fringed shadows on high cheekbones carved from ivory. Utterly lovely, but utterly lifeless. And yet . . . Lewis felt again. Her skin was warm to the touch and her pulse was strong. Her breathing was slow and rhythmic. She seemed to be deep in some kind of trance.

'What have you done to her?' Lewis demanded, his voice, his whole body shaking.

If he had hurt her, harmed her in any way . . . Lewis flushed, the blood throbbing through his cuts and bruising, thudding in his head until he could hardly see, a red film misting the white wall in front of him. His big hands knotted into white knuckled fists. He would destroy Ladslow, break every bone in his body, grind his flesh to pulp . . .

The man read his mind and laughed again, relishing what he found there. Lewis stood up slowly, his fingers uncurling one by one. It was a great effort, but he had to make himself calm down. Chaotic emotion would cloud his judgement, get in his way. Anger was not the answer.

'What have you done to her?' he asked again, his voice betraying just the merest tremor.

'We had a bargain, Lewis.' Ladslow looked at the boy standing before him. 'Don't you remember the first time you came here?'

'I made no bargain with you.' Lewis frowned, trying to

recall just exactly what had been said. It seemed such a long time ago, so much had happened since then . . .

' "Anything" you said,' Ladslow reminded him. ' "I'd give anything" to change. From your former self to what you are now. Anything. I merely took you at your word. We made a bargain. We even shook hands on it. I've just kept my half of it. Look at you, slim, fit, handsome, with money in your pocket and a girlfriend who is beautiful, intelligent and popular and who dotes on you. You don't think those changes are down to you, do you? Due to your own feeble efforts?'

Lewis looked up, about to protest, and met Ladslow's flat black gaze: triumphant, utterly sure. Perhaps the man was right, Lewis thought, perhaps all that had happened had been caused by him. All his old uncertainties came flooding back. He felt diminished.

'It was me,' Ladslow went on, touching his own chest. 'I did it for you. And it is what you wanted, isn't it? Isn't it? "I'd give everything – everything I have – everything I am", that was what you said to me. But I'm not a greedy man,' Ladslow held his hands, palms out, in a gesture of generosity, 'I don't want everything. I only want one little bit.'

'And what would that be?' Lewis asked, his words coming slowly through lips which felt frozen and thick, as though someone else was speaking them.

'Something so small, you can't even see it. Something so intangible most people don't even think they've got one.'

He was still smiling, but his eyes were hard, shiny and black, like marbles. 'I want what you promised to me, Lewis. I want your soul.'

Lewis had not understood before, now he did. In that moment of realisation it all began to make sense to him: the figure of the boy, uncannily lifelike despite his two-thirds size, then the foreign car and the fragment of conversation overheard between Ladslow and the sinister stranger. All the pieces had been there, Lewis had just not put them together – until now.

'Perhaps this will make it clearer.'

Ladslow pulled a sheet back from a space where a bank of shelves and the wall made a little alcove. Lewis did not want to look, he was scared of what would be there, very scared indeed, but he had to see.

Two dolls sat side by side, fingers intertwined, almost life-size. The male figure, the one on the right, was a smaller version of himself. It was dressed like him exactly. The same boots, the same style of shirt, in the same check, the same shade and grade of corduroy in the trousers.

The other doll, the Jennie doll, was also dressed just like the original. Jeans, high-heeled boots, violet long-sleeved T-shirt top; even the shiny silver disc, worn round the neck, was just like the one Lewis had given Jennie last week.

Lewis stared on, fascinated despite his revulsion. The models were exact replicas, but there were subtle differences between them. The Lewis doll looked lifeless, like a waxwork, or a dummy; but there was something different about the other one, the one that looked like Jennie. There was an aura of expectancy about it, as though it might wake at any minute.

Even as Lewis watched, he thought he saw a movement under the eyelid, a tremor along the line of the lashes. He blinked and glanced away, then looked again. Yes, there was a definite stirring. He looked back to the real Jennie, his Jennie. She was still breathing, he could see her chest moving up and down, but she appeared even more pale, even more lifeless. There was a slight upward jerk of the head, her body gave the tiniest shiver, and then she lay still again. It was as if the last essence was draining out of her, as though something, or someone, was stealing the last of her spirit.

'What have you done?' Lewis whispered, appalled, but Ladslow did not seem to hear him.

'As you see, they are not quite finished yet,' Ladslow indicated the replicates. He was drawing from the deep well of his obsession now; it was as if he was conducting a demonstration. 'There are a few adjustments to make, certain final touches which cannot be made without the real subjects.'

He meant the hair. Both of the figures were bald which further subtracted from their human quality, making them grotesque and vulnerable at the same time, like shop window dummies. Lewis's hand strayed to his head, his fingers running through his own thick glossy auburn hair. He remembered Ladslow telling him: 'The best dolls all have human hair', and swallowed down a sudden wave of nausea.

'But why?' he asked. His voice was unsteady. He had trouble getting the words out, but he had to know what was in Ladslow's mind, keep him talking, if he was to find a way out of this madness, if he was to save Jennie.

Ladslow frowned, why couldn't the boy understand? To him, the monstrous was obvious.

'Because,' he sighed, 'doll-making attempts to present an idealised version of life itself. For thousands of years models and replicas have been made with that in mind but, no matter how skilled the maker, dolls cannot move on their own without mechanical means; they cannot speak; they certainly cannot think. That has remained just a dream, the stuff of legend and myth, from Pygmalion and Coppelia to Pinnochio. Until now.' He gazed down at his creations, his black eyes alive with a mixture of affection and pride. 'It has taken me many years and much self-discipline. Much hard study of the arcane, of the occult arts, but now the technique is perfected. I can take the *chi*, life force, soul if you like, of another human being.'

His long thin hands described quick delicate movements in the air and then drew back and into his chest, fingers cupped, forefinger meeting thumb, as if he were miming the movements involved in capturing and holding something.

'I can store it inside myself,' he touched a spot at the centre of his forehead with two fingers, 'and when the time is right, I can transfer it into the figures I make.' He turned his hand, jabbing the two fingers, held in a fork, away from himself. 'Animation in the truest sense.' His eyes became dreamy and distant as he contemplated his own achievement, and then they hardened. 'My product is unique. There are those who will pay a fortune for it. Millions in Swiss francs are being deposited right now in an unmarked bank account.'

'You'll never get away with it!'

'Oh, won't I? I already have – many times!' He laughed, harsh and metallic. 'Think again, Lewis. Take a teenage boy like you.' He smiled, his mouth thin, eyebrows rising. 'Take you. Problems at home, at school—' he waved a hand, describing Lewis's injuries. 'You didn't do that to yourself, did you? What with the enmity of your class mates, and exams coming up – it is all getting too much. Just can't face it any more. No alternative but to run away – as so many do these days. I pick my subjects carefully.'

Lewis looked away from the certainty glowing in Ladslow's eyes. He wasn't lying. He could get away with it, and Lewis knew it. He had read about the cases in the paper, they had even been on TV, but it was only now he was making the connection. That boy they had found, up in Glasgow, he was the skateboarder, the one who used to work here.

'What about Jennie?' he managed to ask.

'Headstrong, impulsive. Running off with her boyfriend like that. Such a foolish thing to do.' Ladslow shrugged, palms up. 'But that's young love for you.'

134

'You still can't—'

'Can't I, though?' Ladslow came closer, hissing the words into Lewis's face. 'I've got witnesses who saw you leave here hours ago and there is nothing to associate Jennie with these premises. She was going to meet you, not me. Mid afternoon was the last anyone saw either of you. You will disappear, forever – just in case the police do try to put two and two together. There will be no mystery bodies. I used to enjoy that part of the game, but this time I will have to employ more caution. No-one will ever find you!' He grinned, absolutely triumphant. 'Cheer up, Lewis!' He clapped the boy on the back. 'It's not all bad.'

'How's that?' Lewis asked, playing for still more time, as his mind raced to measure this man's evil and find a way to combat it.

'You and Jennie will become part of an animated spectacle, you will become the living elements in a tableau vivant. I will call it "The Lovers". Just think, Lewis, you and Jennie will be together, forever. Isn't that what you want? You will stay just as you are now. Never get ugly, never grow older, never tire of each other. Isn't that what you want, too? Isn't that your secret wish? I know it is.' His grin widened, lips drawing back to show wolfish teeth. His eyes gleamed, malicious and evil. 'Apart from being about one third life size, you are both anatomically perfect.'

The idea was deeply sick. The man was clearly insane. Absolutely mad. Crazy to have thought of it in the first place. Even crazier to think he could get away with it. What he described was impossible, a fantasy, it couldn't be done. Lewis clenched his teeth again against a fresh surge of nausea. Ladslow could do it all right. That boy – he might be in hospital somewhere, but Lewis had seen him, or a version of him, here in this very room, sprawled on the floor, looking like he did before, reunited with his property.

Lewis gathered what he could of his strength and prepared to lunge forward and grab for where the throat showed, thin and vulnerable above Ladslow's open-necked shirt.

'Don't even think about it!' Ladslow's voice lost its silky edge, rapping out harsh, echoing in the narrow room, before Lewis could even move. 'There is nothing you can do.'

Lewis stood, held by his gaze, paralysed by the snake-dark eyes, desperately fighting down rising panic as he felt Ladslow's mind sending out probes towards him, seeking to slip inside his consciousness. His only safeguard was to protect his own psyche and keep the invader out. He tried, concentrating his whole being into building up a wall, bringing down the shutters, but one after another every defence was detonated, splintered, blown apart.

'Don't play games with me, Lewis. You are wasting your time. And mine. These pathetic tricks you are trying are things I taught you. And you seek to use them against me?' He laughed. 'They are nothing. As insubstantial as bubbles. You have barely set foot on the path I have trodden all my life. Come now. Don't resist,' his voice was becoming quieter, deeper, sonorous, more and more hypnotic. 'The sooner you give in, the sooner you can join her. Look at me, Lewis. Look at me . . .'

Lewis found himself unable to do anything else. The dark eyes became huge, bigger and bigger, until Lewis thought that he might fall into them. He felt himself becoming lighter and lighter, as if his body would crumple, like so much straw, and his head float away. For a brief moment he glimpsed himself from outside, from above. It was as though his own soul had migrated, to take one last look before saying goodbye.

The whole scene was there, laid out below in exact and minute detail. Himself, motionless and transfixed in front of Ladslow. The man standing there, powerful, gloating, energy pouring from him, flowing out of him in a concentrated beam, bluish white, getting brighter and stronger, like so much plasma. Jennie sprawled against the wall, utterly lifeless now with no movement at all, even the swell and fall of her breathing seemed to have ceased. Over in the corner lay the thing he was destined to be, next to it the other Jennie, the *ka* Jennie, the replicate.

As he looked, it seemed to change. The skin was beginning to flush a delicate pink, the eyelids fluttered, the head turning, as if from sleep. It was becoming animated. Round its neck, resting against the lilac shirt, lay the silver tag that he had given to Jennie. It had their names, hers on the front, his on the back. Ladslow must have stolen it to give to this thing, this replica. What right had he to do that? What right had he to make or break two people's lives, treat them as puppets? Such things were not in his gift. A powerful feeling swelled up in Lewis, not the anger he felt before, but something stronger, deeper, a righteous fury. The creature moved and the medallion flashed, catching the light and throwing it back. Catching the light and throwing it back . . .

Lewis was back in his body. Staring out of his own eyes, gathering himself up inside, mustering all his reserves, focussing all his concentration. This was his last chance, the only chance he had to save himself and Jennie. It would have to be immediate, done in an instant and then over. Complete.

19

'Got a make on the coma case, sir,' PC Sutherland looked down at the fax sheet in front of him. 'James Brindley. Seventeen years old, absconded from a children's home around three years ago, down south somewhere, and hasn't surfaced since. We've still no idea how he got here, we're still working on that, but knowing who he is could be a breakthrough. I thought you'd like to know...'

'Umm,' the doctor continued to stare down at the boy in the bed, he seemed to be hardly listening. The ongoing police investigation had ceased to interest him, all he cared about was his patient. 'Parents?'

The policeman consulted his notes again. 'Mother apparently. Boy went into care because she couldn't cope with him. She's been contacted and is on her way.'

'Hell of a thing.' The doctor rubbed his chin.

'What is?'

'That is. The good news is, we've found your son. Bad news is – how do you feel about organ donation?'

The policeman grinned slightly. Police and medics share

the same black humour. It didn't mean that they didn't care, quite the opposite, but it went with the job, made it bearable.

'Surely it won't come to that?'

'Could do. Since it's only these machines keeping him alive. He can't breathe on his own, can't blink his eyes, can't swallow. A decision will have to be made.'

The policeman looked at the boy. His colour was good. Skin warm to the touch. He appeared quite healthy.

'The boy's dead, essentially,' the doctor went on. 'The brain is not functioning and, without that, this is just a shell, a parody of life we're looking at.' He paused, the wheeze and thunk of the ventilator, the discreet measured beep of the heart monitor seeped into the silence between them. 'Like I said, only the machines are keeping him alive. A decision will have to be made.'

20

Ladslow stood poised, lips parted in a slight smile, eyes wide, body and mind in balanced readiness for the confrontation. The mental conflict, the battle of wills, this had become his favourite part of the whole process. His other subjects had been aimless drifters, with precious little to live for, they gave in with hardly any struggle. The girl had been even less of a challenge. She had been expecting a drink and a chat, not a full blown psychic attack. She had been caught completely off guard; it was over before she knew what was happening.

Lewis was different. An altogether tougher prospect, but still Ladslow did not anticipate too much trouble – just enough to add sauce, a piquant flavour, something to savour. He was confident that he could subdue the boy quickly, bend him to his will, suck out the soul and burn out the mind at precisely the same time. That was how it had worked before, and this would be even more of a reward. After all, he was only harvesting his own, reaping what he had sown.

Lewis watched Ladslow warily, sensing the man was playing with him, and enjoying it; a predator delighting in his power, like a cat with a field mouse. Ladslow was far more powerful, far more practised, he could feel the man's power pulsing towards him, feel his mind circling. A direct confrontation would fail, and Lewis knew it, but he had everything to live for and was prepared to fight. He would marshal all the mental powers, the enormous strength of will that Ladslow had recognised and so carefully fostered, and put them together with a victim's guile, the ingenuity of the weak and small. The old Lewis, despised and bullied, linked with the new.

Lewis held an image in his mind, visualising it placed in the middle of his forehead, like a caste mark, at the centre of command. It started small. Round and flat. The size and brilliance of a new minted ten pence piece, so inconsequential that Ladslow failed to see what the boy was doing at first, but every time he looked back it was bigger: a plate, a paten, a salver. He was trying to create a shield. Ladslow recognised and countered this futile ploy by doubling the mind power he was sending across the room, focussing it into a laser-like intensity, moving in for the kill.

Lewis imagined the disc until it was big enough to cover him and then he set it to spin: her name was on one side, his on the other: Jennie, Lewis, Lewis, Jennie. Round and round it went, faster and faster, until it was a silver blur, showing his name and then hers, a symbol of the love they shared with each other.

Ladslow saw what was happening, but too late. In a fragment of a second he saw how powerful Lewis had become, just how far he had misjudged him. Ladslow smiled. He had chosen this boy precisely because he was clever, because he had shown so much potential. He had chosen well. The boy had developed, grown, changed beyond recognition and Ladslow had helped him. Now he was using Ladslow's own strength against himself and there was nothing he could do. The energy pouring across from him was being caught by the silver spinning disc and was being thrown back, at double, treble, quadruple the force, leaving Ladslow no time to shut down his mind.

He stood for a moment, smiling, unchanged; and then the dark brows arched and bowed in realisation and under them the eyes began to cloud. The twin black centres turned grey and then white, shining, flashing like mirror glasses, reflecting the light. The smile stayed in place for a moment more, frozen in acknowledgement of what had happened, recognising that he had been beaten, then the lips pulled back in a rictus of agony. There was no scream, no sound, as Ladslow fell to the ground.

Lewis came out of his trancelike state to find Ladslow lying at his feet, face down. He knelt over the body, turning it over. Blood trickled from the man's ears, seeping into his beard. His eyes turned up towards the ceiling, bulging white and sightless. Lewis sat back on his heels, hands trembling. He did not want to touch him, but he had to make sure. He felt for the place under the chin. The skin felt cold, clammy to the touch, like chicken skin. Lewis withdrew his hand, wiping his fingers on the knee of his trousers. Ladslow was dead. There was no pulse whatsoever. No pulse at all.

Ladslow had stolen Jennie's soul, taken it into himself. If the puppet master dies, what becomes of the puppet? The thought tore into Lewis, shattering what was left of his resolve and courage. He closed his eyes, tears squeezing through the lashes. He dare not look. He did not want to see what had happened to Jennie. Was she lying lifeless, soulless as a replicate? Was she on her way to hell, joined for eternity to Ladslow's black soul?

'What am I doing here?'

The voice from the corner sounded thin and faint, high and hesitant, as if speech was new to it. Still Lewis could not look round.

'Lewis?'

The hand touching his bowed head, the back of his neck, was human, the skin pliant and warm. He turned and saw Jennie's own green eyes looking into his.

'Something happened . . .' she frowned. 'I don't remember . . .' then her whole face changed, contracting in horror, as she took in the prone figure of Ladslow. 'What's going on here?'

'Ladslow seems to have had some kind of seizure.'

'Shouldn't we call an ambulance, or something?'

Jennie looked round vaguely, still trying to gather her scattered wits together. Then her hand went to her mouth.

She was staring into the corner, pointing at the replicates. She lurched sideways, and would have fallen if Lewis had not steadied her. A sensation, as of extreme vertigo, gripped her. A feeling of falling and falling into a void, a black pit of emptiness, of dreadful aloneness, of being forever lost.

'What . . .' she managed to whisper. 'What are those?'

'I don't know. Not exactly . . .' Lewis shook his head. The likeness was still there, but the similarity was fading, waning. The figures lay stiff-limbed, plastic and lifeless, like an over-sized Ken and Barbie, only the clothes held any resemblance to themselves. 'Are you all right?'

'Yes, I think so. Now.' She turned back to Lewis, suddenly noticing his face, the scratching and bruising.

'Lewis! Your face! What happened to your face?'

'I'll tell you later. Come on,' Lewis struggled to his feet. 'Let's get out of here.'

Far to the north, a nurse looked up, alerted by a choking noise coming from the bed. He was regaining consciousness. He was coming round. She acted quickly, hurrying to remove the plastic tube from his windpipe. As she worked, the eyes opened and stared up at her, blue and unfocussed, and then looked about, slowly taking in the surroundings.

'Who are you?' he managed to say, once his mouth was free from tubing. 'Where am I? What has happened to me?'

The nurse shook her head, too full of emotion to say anything.

21

Lewis and Jennie waited outside until an ambulance and police car arrived. The light bars stayed on as the men went in.

'He's dead, son,' one of the ambulance men said when he came out, but Lewis didn't need telling.

'You find him?' the police constable asked.

Lewis nodded.

'We'll need a statement.' Lewis inclined his head and the constable turned from him to the ambulance man. 'What do you reckon?'

'Don't know. Hard to tell.' The man looked at his mate and they both shrugged. 'But it looks like natural causes. Stroke, most probably . . .'

The policeman agreed. It seemed that way to him, too. No sign of assault, or a break in, nothing like that. The day's takings were still in the till, and they amounted to quite a substantial sum of money. There would have to be some kind of investigation, but it would be just a formality, going through the motions more than anything. It all seemed quite straightforward.

'And you've no idea how it happened?' He was talking to Lewis and Jennie now. 'Just found him like that?'

The girl assented, but Lewis was not looking at him, he was too busy watching the light from the ambulance flash blue and white on the glass of the darkened window. It reminded him of eyes . . .

'What about you, son?'

'Oh, yes, that's right.' Lewis turned to the policeman. 'We just went back there, to collect my wages, that's when we found him. We've got no idea what happened to him, no idea at all.'

On the way home, he told Jennie what had happened, or what he thought had happened, but the events became less real as he described them, until they seemed like a dream, even to him. Jennie listened carefully, questioning now and again, asking for clarification. When he had finished, she merely nodded. It did not make sense, not in any rational way, but she knew the truth of what he was saying; she had been there, she had felt it inside her. Some things are too deep for reason.

'You don't think he was right, do you?' he asked after a while.

One of the things Ladslow had said remained with him, caught like a barb in his brain, already setting up infection, getting more deeply embedded the more he tried to get rid of it.

'About what?'

'About, you know, him changing me. Doing it for me. Making me different from what I was before. Turning me from the fat kid who nobody liked, to, well, what I am now. And you, too,' his voice dropped to a whisper. 'What if he put some kind of spell on you. I mean, I thought, I thought, you loved me for myself, but what if I'm wrong? What if none of it was down to me at all.'

Jennie stopped walking and looked up at him.

'No, Lewis. You can't believe that, not for a minute, because it's not true. If it was,' she shuddered, 'we would be on our way to Switzerland in whatever form he cared to put us in. You stopped him. You defeated him. You did that yourself.'

'Yes, but—'

'But nothing. Believe it, Lewis. You have to. If you doubt yourself now, he'll . . .' Jennie broke off.

'He'll what?'

Jennie's voice dropped. 'He'll have won. It will be his victory. Anyway,' she said after a bit, 'I don't see it like that.'

'Like what?'

'Like you've changed. I think it's more like you found yourself, let your true self come out. And as for him putting a spell on me,' she shook her head, 'that's just silly. I always liked you, Lewis. You were always good, always kind. I would have loved you – should have loved you, anyway – if I hadn't been too blind to see what you were really like underneath. When I think about Ross, that I ever preferred him to you – it makes me go cold inside. What I feel now,

149

what I think, never had anything to do with Ladslow.'

Jennie took his hand and they walked on in silence. There was no need to talk any more, they did not have to, the bond was strong between them. Lewis had come back for her, and he had saved her, but only Jennie knew from what. She had been the one to have life force stripped out of her to become an empty shell, filled with black nothingness. Only she knew what it was like to wander, lost and bereft, in an infinity of endless space. Only she knew what it was to live without a soul.

22

Ladslow's shop remained closed for a long time, but eventually some distant relative turned up to claim his inheritance. Shop and stock were sold off and the place turned over to new ownership. It became a kitchen shop, part of a chain. People looking for toys had to go to one of the big out of town stores. Another part of the town's heritage gone.

Lewis always looked into the shop when he crossed the square, no matter what was on display there. Sometimes he would stop and think about Ladslow and wonder what had twisted him, what had happened to warp his brilliance and turn it into evil. Lewis had trusted him at first, respected him, even liked him, and he had seen those feelings turn through 360 degrees to fear, horror and loathing. Now he did not feel anything. He just remembered the man who had changed his own life forever. And for the better. Sometimes it happens like that: good can come out of bad.

He and Jennie were still together, at the sixth form college now. He was doing well on his A level courses, and things had settled down at home. They were by no means perfect, but Dad seemed reconciled to changes he could do nothing about; and his mum had taken a leaf out of her son's book, joining a diet group, going to aerobics, really sticking at it. She'd even got a job in a wool and knitwear shop, and could buy anything she liked now, and she had a new hair style, new clothes – you name it – she was going from strength to strength.

Lewis would stay in front of the shop for a while, think about it all, thinking about what had happened to him and, just for a second, the window would fill with big orange pumpkin lantern balloons and Halloween faces. He would feel someone searching, reaching out for him. Maybe it was the angle of his gaze, or a trick of the light on a reflective surface, but he'd look back and find that one of the masks was different from the others, dark-haired and bearded, with eyes as bright as mirror lenses, and Ladslow would be there looking at him, right in the middle of the window.

ORDER FORM

Celia Rees

0 340 81800 X	CITY OF SHADOWS	£5.99	❏
0 340 81801 8	A TRAP IN TIME	£5.99	❏
0 340 81802 6	THE HOST RIDES OUT	£5.99	❏

All Hodder Children's books are available at your local bookshop, or can be ordered direct from the publisher. Just tick the titles you would like and complete the details below. Prices and availability are subject to change without prior notice.

Please enclose a cheque or postal order made payable to *Bookpoint Ltd*, and send to: Hodder Children's Books, 39 Milton Park, Abingdon, OXON OX14 4TD, UK.
Email Address: orders@bookpoint.co.uk

If you would prefer to pay by credit card, our call centre team would be delighted to take your order by telephone. Our direct line *01235 400414* (lines open 9.00 am–6.00 pm Monday to Saturday, 24 hour message answering service). Alternatively you can send a fax on *01235 400454*.

TITLE		FIRST NAME		SURNAME	

ADDRESS	
DAYTIME TEL:		POST CODE	

If you would prefer to pay by credit card, please complete:
Please debit my Visa/Access/Diner's Card/American Express (delete as applicable) card no:

Signature .... Expiry Date: ....

If you would NOT like to receive further information on our products please tick the box.   ❏